World's Most
Eligible Bachelors

Gina Wilkins

Doctor in Disguise

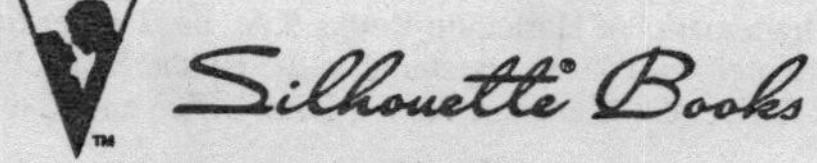

Published by Silhouette Books
America's Publisher of Contemporary Romance

For my daughter, Kerry, whose idea of a fun summer is crawling on her belly through cave mud. Thanks for helping me with my research.

SILHOUETTE BOOKS

ISBN 0-373-65024-8

DOCTOR IN DISGUISE

This edition published by arrangement with Harlequin Books S.A.

Printed in U.S.A.

A Conversation with...
Award-winning author
GINA WILKINS

What hero have you created for WORLD'S MOST ELIGIBLE BACHELORS, and how has he earned the coveted title?

GW: Alexander Keating is a nationally renowned cardiologist who has money, a degree of fame, an impeccable family lineage and a coveted place in New England society—all of which make him a World's Most Eligible Bachelor. But it was the kindness and compassion beneath that polished facade that made him *my* pick.

What about WORLD'S MOST ELIGIBLE BACHELORS appealed to you?

GW: I was intrigued by this series because part of the universal appeal of romance novels is taking those wonderful, larger-than-life, confirmed-bachelor heroes and watching what happens when they tumble reluctantly into love. All of the men in this series have been highly successful in their careers, but there is something still lacking in their lives. A soul mate.

What modern-day personality best epitomizes a WORLD'S MOST ELIGIBLE BACHELOR?

GW: The renowned "personalities" I most admire tend to be *former* "Eligible Bachelors"—men who have proven to be devoted and faithful husbands to the women they married. A true romance hero is a man who falls in love for life, and who never breaks the vows of commitment he makes to his mate. My own husband is this kind of "hero," and for twenty-two years I have never doubted his loyalty or his commitment to me or to our three children.

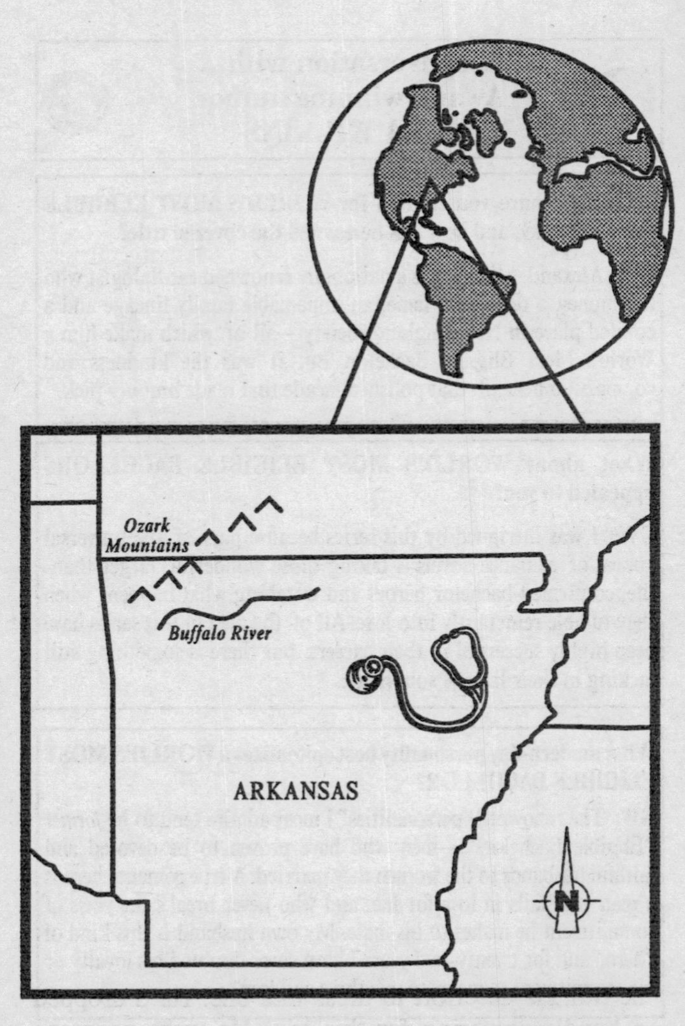
Ozark
Mountains
Buffalo River
ARKANSAS
N

One

On the afternoon of his fortieth birthday, Robert Alexander Keating Jr. stood knee-deep in a chilly north Arkansas river, a nine-foot graphite fly rod in his hand and a contented smile on his face beneath a two-day growth of beard. Alex was alone on this momentous Wednesday in September. He had awakened alone that morning and would sleep alone that night. There would be no banners or balloons, no birthday cake or candles, no gifts or guests or champagne.

And best of all, it would be very unlikely that he would run into anyone who had seen him featured in that World's Most Eligible Bachelor article in *Prominence Magazine.* None of his friends to continue their teasing, none of the women who seemed determined to take him off the bachelor list—whether he was interested or not.

He was spending this day exactly the way he wanted to.

With a splash, a trout broke the surface of the river three yards from where Alex was fishing. He hadn't even had a nibble so far on the fly he'd been using. He wondered if he should switch to a mayfly, but decided to try the nymph awhile longer.

Alex was hardly an expert fly fisherman, though he'd made an effort to dress like one. He'd dropped a bundle preparing for this trip. He wore neoprene bootfoot waders with felt soles and a two-hundred-dollar fishing vest, pockets stuffed with fly boxes, tippet spools, fly floatant and other fishing necessities. Fancy clippers hung from a pin-on reel on his left shoulder, a hemostat was clipped to the inside of the vest and a landing net dangled from a ring high on his back. His felt-brimmed hat looked too new to mark him as a seasoned pro. Polarized glasses protected his eyes from the sun and gave him better visibility of the fish beneath the surface—not that seeing them equated with catching them, in his case.

The fact that he hadn't yet hooked any fish didn't bother him in the least. He had the musical sound of rushing water to entertain him. The rustling of breeze-blown leaves. The melody of birds singing in the treetops.

It was the second day of the first vacation Alex had taken in years. For the next two weeks—and for the first time in almost longer than he could remember—he was unreachable by telephone, pager, E-mail or intercom.

Alex had been so busy saving lives during the past fifteen years that he'd almost forgotten how to enjoy his own.

The strike indicator on his leader disappeared, and in his excitement at having a bite, he overreacted. The fish got away—probably laughing at the amateur on the other end of the line, Alex thought ruefully. And then he grinned and started pulling in his line, eager to try again.

He wondered what his acquaintances at home would think if they could see him now.

When he finally landed a good-sized brown trout,

it was with a surge of satisfaction that made his breath catch.

"Look at you," he murmured, cradling the visibly annoyed fish carefully in his hands. "You're beautiful."

The trout bucked, obviously unswayed by the compliment.

Chuckling, Alex steadied the fish beneath the water, reassured himself that it was rested and ready to swim, then let it go. The trout disappeared upstream with a defiant flick of its tail.

Still kneeling, Alex watched it swim away. Damn, but he felt good. He should have done something like this a long time ago. Giving in to a rare, exuberant impulse, he stood and punched the air with a jubilant whoop.

Startled by the sudden noise slicing through the formerly peaceful afternoon, a deer that had been hiding by the riverbank bounded into sight. Jumping and crashing through the brush, it dashed away.

Alex was caught completely off guard. He turned too quickly on the wet rocks that made up the riverbed. One foot slid from beneath him. Struggling to hold on to his seven-hundred-dollar rod and reel, he lost his balance and fell heavily. There was a moment of blinding pain when his head struck a large rock, and then blackness.

His last thought as he slid into unconsciousness was that at least he'd died happy.

Alex woke in the back of a pickup. A deeply tanned, grizzled-looking man of about sixty knelt beside him, studying him with curious, concerned eyes.

"I think he's comin' round," he said, obviously not talking to Alex.

Another man of about the same age as the first climbed into the truck bed. Seeing that Alex's eyes were open, he touched a callused finger to the brim of his cap and said, "Don't you worry now. We've brought you to see Dr. Fletcher. You'll be fixed up in no time."

"I, uh—"

Alex had wanted to protest that he didn't need a doctor, that he *was* a doctor, but his tongue didn't seem to be working right.

"You get on his right side, Burle, and I'll get the left," the second man instructed.

While Alex was still trying to formulate a coherent sentence, the two men took hold of him and slid him off the tailgate, balancing him between them once they reached the ground. The small, natural-stone building in front of them bore a sign identifying it as a medical clinic.

Alex was cold, wet, dizzy and confused, and his head was throbbing. He could feel something warm and sticky dripping from his forehead, and he knew he must look like a horror-movie extra. But he still didn't relish the thought of being examined by a backwoods country doctor. If only his tongue would cooperate with his brain so that he could get out the words.

He wasn't given the chance to say anything. The two outdoorsy-looking men who had brought him to this place hauled him forward, steadying him with work-strengthened arms when he swayed on his feet.

His hat and glasses were gone. His fishing vest was dripping, and he couldn't feel his net hanging from the ring on the back. His neoprene waders were filled with water. God only knew what had happened to his seven-hundred-dollar rod and reel.

His perfect day had taken a sharp downhill turn.

A woman greeted them when they shuffled through the door of the clinic into a no-frills waiting room. Alex noted in one rather bleary glance that she appeared to be in her late twenties or early thirties, that her layered, shoulder-length hair was dark blond and her eyes a rich, chocolate brown. She was of average height and build and was wearing jeans, a plaid cotton shirt with a denim collar and a white lab coat.

"Looks like someone took a fall in the river," she remarked with a warm smile for Alex.

Assuming the woman was a nurse, Alex tried to reply. "I...uh..."

The man who'd been identified as Burle chuckled. "That's all he's managed to say since we found him. I think he rattled his brains some, Doc."

Alex resented that. There was nothing wrong with his brain. It was his tongue that was giving him trouble. And had Burle called this woman "Doc"?

Confirming that Alex had heard correctly, the woman introduced herself. "I'm Dr. Carly Fletcher," she said. "Come on back and I'll take a look at that lump on your head."

"She's a good doctor," Burle murmured into Alex's ear. "Don't let her being a woman put you off none, you hear?"

Alex might have been wryly amused had his head not been pounding so violently. He might have even quipped that some of his best friends were women doctors. As it was, he could only swallow a groan and put himself into this particular woman doctor's hands.

"Well," Carly said after swiftly and efficiently examining the wet, bloody man who'd been brought into her office only moments before she'd intended to leave for the day, "you've whacked your head a good one."

Despite his obvious discomfort, the man's firm mouth quirked into a crooked smile. "Is that your professional opinion, Doctor?" he asked, his voice a bit thick but finally coherent.

Surprised by the unexpected east coast accent, Carly looked a bit more closely at her patient's features. Beneath the mud and gore, he was quite handsome, with hair that was either black or very dark brown—hard to tell until it dried—and eyes such a dark blue they could almost be called navy.

"Yes," she said with a smile. "That is my professional opinion. What's your name?" she asked, swabbing at the rapidly bruising cut on his right temple.

"Alex Keating."

"Vacationing in this area, Mr. Keating?"

"Yes. I was doing some fishing."

"Trying to catch them with your hands, were you?" she asked dryly.

His smile deepened. "No. With my head."

"Around here, folks usually try a rod and reel."

"I'll keep that in mind."

Carly chuckled and continued her job.

Ten minutes later, she stepped back and nodded. "The cut at your temple is shallow enough that it doesn't need stitches. I've applied a butterfly bandage, and I expect it to heal without a scar. As for the lump behind your right ear, it's going to be sore for a few days. It's possible that you have a mild concussion, but your pupils are responding well, your blood pressure is fine, and now that you're talking, I see no evidence of serious trauma. Is there someone who can check on you a couple of times during the night?''

''No, I'm vacationing alone. But I'll be fine,'' he assured her without evidence of concern.

Carly frowned. ''Where are you staying?''

''One of the fishing cabins along the river.''

''Is there a phone?''

''No.''

She shook her head. ''I'm not comfortable with that at all. Brain injuries, even the slight bruising of a mild concussion, are nothing to fool around with, Mr. Keating. You were in and out of consciousness for a little more than ten minutes, according to Burle and Jeff, and disoriented after you regained full consciousness. At least for tonight, I would like someone to keep an eye on you.''

''I'll be fine,'' he repeated. ''I've had some experience with this sort of thing. I know what to watch for.''

Carly had encountered stubborn patients—mostly men—before. She knew how to handle them. With firmness. ''That's a risk I'm simply not willing to take. We'll have to make other arrangements for you tonight.''

He shook his head, obviously prepared to argue. The jarring motion must have set off an explosion of pain. She watched as he paled and swayed on the examining table.

Quickly, Carly put out a hand to steady him. ''See

what I mean?'' she asked gently. ''Looks like you'll be getting a taste of Southern hospitality tonight, Mr. Keating. You can stay at my place.''

He blinked rapidly a few times, looking at her in surprise. ''At your place?'' he repeated, as if he weren't sure he'd heard her correctly.

''Yes. It's quiet there, just me and my grandmother. There's a spare bedroom with its own bath, so you won't be in our way. I'll check on you a couple of times during the night, and then, if you're feeling better tomorrow, you can go back to your fishing cabin and your solitude.''

He shook his head again, more carefully this time. ''You can't just take a strange man into your home,'' he said in disapproval.

She lifted an eyebrow, amused at his warning. ''Oh? Just how strange *are* you?''

He frowned at her. ''I'm not joking. What if I were a rapist? Or a thief?''

''If you're a thief, you won't get much at my place,'' she replied ruefully. ''Country doctors in financially strapped areas don't exactly get rich. And would a deranged rapist really warn me about the danger of taking him home with me?''

''How would I know that?'' Alex Keating asked crossly.

''You would if you were one,'' she retorted. ''Mr. Keating, I can't insist that you accept my offer, of course. But I really wish you would consider it. It's only for one night, and you don't want to take a reckless chance with your health, do you? The standard treatment for a mild concussion is to monitor for signs of intracranial bleeding and pressure, and I'm trained to do that. Will you allow me to do my job tonight?''

She watched as he seemed to debate her question inside his obviously aching head. And then he nodded—slowly, as if afraid his head might roll right off his neck if he moved too quickly. "Thank you," he said a bit gruffly. "I appreciate the offer."

"Just think of it as a reverse house call," she said, relieved that he'd agreed. "Is that painkiller having any effect yet?"

"Maybe a little," he said cautiously, lifting one hand to the lump at his temple.

Noting that his hand wasn't quite steady, Carly took his arm. "Let me help you out to my truck," she said. "I'll run you by the cabin so you can get a few of your things."

"What about the men who brought me here?"

"I sent them home. They knew I would take care of you. By the way, Burle told me that they put all your fishing gear in the back of my truck. He figured I'd be taking you somewhere after I treated you."

"You people are certainly trusting of strangers," her patient murmured, still looking faintly disapproving.

"You think so?" Carly smiled, musing that Alex Keating had a great deal to learn about the people of the Arkansas Ozarks area. But he was in no shape to try to understand the complexities of the region or its people now. He was chilled, wet and in pain, and Carly thought that what he needed most was a change of clothing, hot food and drink and a warm bed.

"Lean on me, Mr. Keating," she said, offering a shoulder. "I'll take good care of you."

Alex had been all set to renew his arguments that he was perfectly capable of taking care of himself once he was back in the comfort of his rented cabin. But by the time he'd managed to change into dry clothes a short time later, he was so shaky that he knew he would never convince the ultradedicated Dr. Fletcher that he was operating at full capacity.

If only he could get those jackhammers out of his head, he thought, making his way carefully into the main room, where she waited for him.

She had been standing by the window, watching the sun set on the river just visible through the fall-colored trees. She turned with a smile when Alex joined her. "Do you have everything? Is there anything I can do to help?"

He held up the overnight bag in his left hand. "I have everything I need for one night. But look, Dr. Fletcher, I'm feeling much better. I've got food and a bed here, and the chances are slim that any serious complications will develop from my bump on the head. So there's really no need—"

She broke in with a quick laugh. "You are the independent type, aren't you, Mr. Keating? Is it so hard for you to accept a helping hand just for one night? And as far as possible complications go, who's the doctor here—you or me?" she demanded with teasing severity.

He thought seriously about answering that they were *both* doctors. That Dr. Robert Alexander Keating was a highly respected Boston cardiologist accustomed to medical facilities that made Carly's little backwoods clinic look like a primitive witch doctor's hut. But that would be a churlish thing to say to someone who was only trying to help him, and despite his rapidly worsening headache and the accompanying bad mood, he wouldn't sink to that level. For now, he'd rather keep his profession to himself.

"Okay, fine. Whatever you think best, Doctor."

"There," she said in satisfaction. "Was that so hard?"

Actually, he'd found it a very enlightening experience. He'd discovered that he didn't much care to be at the receiving end of a doctor's orders.

Even a doctor as attractive and pleasant as this one, he thought ruefully.

With the no-nonsense manner he'd come to expect from her, she stuffed him back into her dual-cab red 4x4 pickup and drove him to her home some fifteen miles away. They left his rental car behind, since Alex was in no shape to drive. She promised to return him to his cabin the next morning.

Her house, a pretty, two-story yellow frame with a big, inviting front porch, was located on a gravel road nestled into a scenic hollow. There was only one other house visible, a one-story gray brick on the other side of the road. Both houses had long driveways, large, tree-filled yards and functional-looking outbuildings.

"Nice," Alex murmured, turning his aching head cautiously to look around as Carly turned into her driveway.

"Thanks. I called my grandmother on my cell phone while you were changing. She's expecting us."

Alex wanted to be back in his cabin, alone, where he could take something for his headache, crawl into bed and pull the covers over his head for about twelve hours. This was not at all the way he had intended to spend his vacation. He was feeling more stupid by the minute.

And now he had to go make nice with the good doctor's grandma.

He made his way to the front door without assistance, feeling a little stronger despite the headache that was reverberating through his skull. Dr. Fletcher followed close on his heels, available, but casual about it.

The front door opened before they reached it. A gray-haired woman with kind, bright eyes and a friendly smile greeted them. There was no doubt that this was Carly's grandmother; the family resemblance was striking despite the large difference in age.

"You must be Mr. Keating. I'm Betty Fletcher. Goodness gracious, that's a nasty bump on your head! Must hurt like the dickens."

"Well, yes, as a matter of fact..."

"Get on in here and sit down. Let me get you something to drink. Are you a coffee man or would you rather have tea?"

"Um...tea, please." And a nice, quiet, private room to drink it in, he wanted to add.

Instead, Mrs. Fletcher ushered Alex into a fussy living room and installed him on a deep-cushioned sofa before bustling away to fetch his tea. Carly ran a hand through her tousled layers of dark blond hair. "I haven't been home since six this morning," she said. "Almost thirteen hours. I'd like to go freshen up. If you need anything, please feel free to tell my grandmother."

"I'll be fine, thank you."

Her chocolate eyes were too perceptive when they swept his face. Her smile held a touch of sympathy. "What you'd really like," she murmured, "is for these pushy strangers to leave you alone, right?"

He cleared his throat. "I didn't say that."

"No, but it's what I'd be thinking if I were in your shoes. I've never liked being hovered over, either."

Rubbing his uninjured temple, Alex looked at his hostess more closely. She really did have beautiful eyes, he mused. And a fresh, unpretentious smile that tempted him to smile back despite his mood. There wasn't a hint of flirtation in her friendly, plainspoken manner toward him, and that, too, was refreshing—especially since the publication of that ridiculous magazine article about him a few months earlier.

Prominence Magazine had decided, because of his illustrious family name, their tidy fortune and his own noted success in the field of cardiology, to include him on the list of the world's twelve most eligible bachelors—and since then he'd become one of the most hounded!

Maybe that was one of the reasons he found himself so enjoying Carly's company. She wasn't his usual type—whatever that was—but something about Dr. Carly Fletcher appealed quite strongly to Alex. Or was it only his head injury making him respond so forcefully and so uncharacteristically to her?

Before he could formulate an answer, Carly left the room and her grandmother came back in, carrying a cup of hot tea with the tag from a tea bag still dangling down one side of the cup. "Do you want it sweetened?" she asked, setting the cup carefully on the oak coffee table in front of Alex. "I have real sugar or some of that artificial stuff that Carly uses, if you prefer."

"I'll take it straight, thanks." Alex set the dripping tea bag on the saucer she'd provided and took a sip.

He felt the warmth seeping into his weary body, gradually easing his pounding headache.

Mrs. Fletcher didn't linger for small talk but hurried away to set dinner on the table, leaving Alex a few moments of grateful solitude. He drank his tea and then leaned his head back against the sofa, eyes closed, forcing his taut muscles to relax.

By the time his hostesses invited him to join them in the dining room for dinner, he was feeling almost human again. And by the time he'd eaten a light meal of homemade vegetable soup and corn bread, he was almost glad that Carly had insisted on bringing him home with her.

Carly and her grandmother talked quietly through the meal, letting Alex eat in peace. Apparently, Carly made a practice of telling her grandmother about her day during dinner, and several times she made Mrs. Fletcher laugh aloud at innocuous anecdotes about mutual acquaintances.

Mrs. Fletcher eventually turned to Alex. "How are you feeling, Mr. Keating?"

He nodded tentatively, realizing that he could do so now without feeling as if his head were going to fall off his shoulders. "Better, thank you. Dinner was delicious, Mrs. Fletcher."

"Call me Betty," she instructed him. "Everyone does, except Carly. She calls me Granny."

"And I'm Alex."

"Do you feel up to dessert, Alex? I have cherry cobbler," Betty said enticingly.

His smile felt crooked. "That sounds great, but I really don't think I can hold any more right now."

Carly looked at him swiftly. "Nausea?"

He wasn't accustomed to being seen by an attractive woman as nothing more than a patient, a set of symptoms. And for some reason, he didn't like it, especially from this particular woman. But he managed to reply politely enough. "No. I'm just not hungry."

"Is your head still hurting? Any blurring of your vision?"

"I'm fine." Aware that his answer had been a bit curt that time, he added, "Thank you."

To his surprise, Betty reached over and patted his hand. "You don't like being a patient, do you, Alex? My late husband was the same way. He just hated admitting when he was feeling poorly."

Not quite certain how to answer, Alex only cleared his throat.

A few minutes later, Carly showed Alex to the guest bedroom. It was a nice-sized room, decorated in heavy oak furniture and dark-colored linens and draperies. She pointed out a television set in an oak cabinet, a selection of hardback books in a built-in bookcase and the door to the private attached bath.

"This is the room my brothers use when they visit—which isn't often," she explained with a smile.

"Brothers?"

"Three of them. Two older, one younger." She headed for the door without pausing to chat further. "I'll be in a couple of times during the night to check on you. Don't hesitate to ask if you need anything—food, drink, pain medication, whatever."

"Dr. Fletcher?"

She turned at the doorway. "Carly," she corrected him. "We're an informal household."

He nodded. "I just wanted to thank you. It's very kind of you to be so concerned about my welfare."

She looked just a bit disconcerted. "You're here alone, and you've been injured. What else could I have done?"

"You could have expected me to fend for myself. You had no obligation to take me in."

She shrugged. "I feel a certain responsibility for all my patients."

Even if she was telling him that he shouldn't take her generosity personally, Alex still thought it was remarkable that she'd gone to so much trouble for a man who was a complete stranger to her. Never in his career had he ever taken one of his patients home with him, he thought after Carly closed the door behind her. It would never have even occurred to him to do so.

More tired than he should have been, he stripped out of his clothes, donning a T-shirt and sweatpants to wear to bed, since Carly would be in to monitor him during the night. He washed his face and brushed his teeth, then thought briefly about turning on the television. But the big bed looked very inviting, and he couldn't resist crawling into it. He was asleep almost before his head hit the pillow.

He hadn't gone to bed that early since grade school. The fact that he fell asleep so quickly and so deeply had as much to do with his long-denied need for rest as it did with the bump on his head.

Alex's sleep was disturbed twice during the night. The first time it was Carly, who woke him to check his pupils and ask him if he needed anything for pain. Squinting against the light from the bedside lamp, Alex declined the medication, assured her that he was fine and thanked her for her concern.

He went back to sleep wondering what Carly had been wearing beneath the white terry-cloth robe that had covered her from throat to toes.

The next time a soft hand touched his forehead, his first thought was that Carly had returned. He was rather surprised that she chose to wake him this time with a tender touch.

He opened his eyes, squinted into the light and was even more surprised to find that it wasn't Carly at all but her grandmother leaning over him.

"How are you feeling, Alex?" she asked, as if he were a sick boy rather than a forty-year-old man.

"Much better, thank you." His voice was still husky from sleep as he answered candidly. His headache was gone, he was feeling much less sore, and he was confident that he was well on the way to a full recovery.

"Good. Do you need anything? Are you warm enough? Are you thirsty?"

"I'm fine, Betty," he assured her.

"Then I'll let you go back to sleep. Good night, dear."

Dear. It was what his own grandmother had always called him.

It had been a very long time since anyone had taken care of Alex. And it felt pretty good for a change, he admitted to himself as he drifted back to sleep.

Two

Recovered enough to feel foolish again for his careless fall, Alex made his way downstairs the next morning in search of his hostesses. He intended to thank them for their generous hospitality, find out what he owed the doctor for her services, assure them he was quite capable of taking care of himself from now on, and then beg a ride back to his rented cabin.

Alone in the kitchen, Betty greeted him with a smile. "Good morning. How do you feel?"

"Fine, thank you."

"Hungry?"

The smells of coffee and fresh-baked pastries were already making Alex's mouth water. "Yes, as a matter of fact, I am."

"Sit down," she urged. "I'll fix your plate."

"Is there anything I can do to help you?"

"No, you just sit. I've got everything ready."

Once again, Alex was forcibly reminded of his late grandmother. She, too, had seemed happiest when she was feeding someone...usually him.

He noted that Betty prepared only one plate, which she set in front of him. "Have you and Carly eaten?"

"I waited so you wouldn't have to eat alone," Betty replied, pulling another plate out of the pantry for herself. "Carly had to leave on an emergency call very early this morning. Heaven only knows when she'll get a chance to grab a bite, poor girl."

"Is she the only doctor working in her clinic?"

"The only doctor within a twenty-mile radius," Betty explained. "She stays very busy."

Alex stayed incredibly busy himself. So much so that he hardly knew how to relax anymore. Still, his practice was quite specialized, and he had the support of a large, quickly mobilized medical staff. Carly had to be prepared to deal with anything, and to do so on her own. He'd never really given much thought to what the life of a rural general practitioner must be like.

Betty chatted brightly while they ate breakfast, talking mostly about her granddaughter. Her pride in Carly was obvious as she explained that Carly had wanted to be a doctor since she was very young. Coming from a family of very modest means, Carly had to work hard to put herself through college and medical school. She'd had financial assistance from a foundation dedicated to placing primary care physicians in underserved communities, and she took that obligation very seriously, Betty explained.

Carly had bought the clinic in tiny Seventy-Six, Arkansas, five years ago from a doctor who'd served the community for more than forty years. It had taken the locals a short while to get used to having a woman doctor, but Carly had earned their acceptance, their respect, and then their friendship.

Carly's staff, according to Betty, consisted of a "dear young woman" who manned the desk at the clinic, a "grumpy but good-hearted" full-time L.P.N., and an R.N. who worked three days a week. Many of her patients were poor and underinsured. Carly had been paid for her services in home-cooked meals, plumbing and electrical work, car repairs and crayon drawings, Betty added with a smile, but she loved her work and the community she served. She got by on what she earned from her paying customers and from insurance and Medicaid and Medicare reimbursements, but money wasn't what had brought Carly into medicine in the first place.

"She has a need to help people," Betty said. "A real calling to ease their pain."

"You don't have to convince me that Carly is extraordinary. Not after all she did for me yesterday."

Betty nodded, apparently satisfied that he properly appreciated her beloved granddaughter.

"Has Carly lived with you ever since she went into practice for herself?" Alex asked, wondering about the attractive young doctor's social life.

"Carly doesn't live with me, Alex. I live with her," Betty corrected gently. "She bought this house when she moved here five years ago. She insisted that I move in with her after my husband passed away three years later."

"She must have graduated medical school very young."

Betty smiled. "She's a bit older than she looks. She's thirty-four."

"You're right. She looks younger," Alex concurred, picturing Carly's pretty, unlined face.

"How old are *you,* Alex?"

Amused by the blatantly personal question, Alex answered honestly. "As of yesterday, I'm forty."

Betty's eyes widened. "Yesterday was your birthday?"

"Yes. This fishing trip was a birthday present to

myself.'' He touched the still-swollen lump on his head. ''I didn't plan for this, of course,'' he added wryly.

''Didn't you want to spend your birthday with your family?'' Betty seemed scandalized by the idea that he'd been alone on such an occasion.

''My parents are spending the winter in Italy,'' he explained. ''They left last week. We had a birthday dinner the night before their departure.''

''And you have no other family?''

''Just my parents.''

Betty studied him closely. ''I'm surprised a good-looking young man like you doesn't have a wife and children.''

Her comments might have been considered intrusive in Alex's Boston circles. But from the experience he had with this part of the country, and with senior citizens who were beyond worrying about political correctness, Betty's open curiosity was no great shock.

''No wife. No kids,'' he said easily. ''I guess you could say I've been married to my work.''

Clicking her tongue in disapproval, Betty shook her head. ''I figured you were one of those high-powered businessmen when you told us last night that you were from Boston. How long has it been since you've had a vacation?''

''Longer than I can remember,'' he admitted. He wasn't sure why he was being so evasive about the nature of his work. It just seemed easier not to mention it.

''Just as I thought. And how long are you planning to stay in our area?''

"I had planned on two full weeks. Yesterday was my second day."

"I hope your little accident hasn't ruined your enjoyment of your visit."

"No, not at all," he assured her. And was almost surprised to realize that he meant it.

"Would you like anything more to eat?" she asked, drawing his attention to the fact that he'd completely cleaned his plate.

He shook his head, pleased that it no longer hurt to do so. "No, thank you. Maybe another cup of coffee, though."

"Help yourself. Feel free to take it into the living room while I clean up in here. Today's newspaper's on the coffee table, or you're welcome to turn on the TV, if you like. Carly said she'd be back as soon as possible to take you to your fishing cabin when you're ready."

Alex knew he should be in a hurry to leave, to get back to the solitude he'd craved, but for some reason he was perfectly content to be where he was at the moment. Maybe, he thought, sipping from his freshly filled mug, it had something to do with Betty Fletcher being such a great cook. It had been a long time since Alex had enjoyed a home-cooked breakfast.

"I think I'll drink this on the front porch," he said, remembering the big, inviting rockers he'd spotted there last night.

Betty nodded approval. "It's a beautiful morning. Take a little walk around if you like."

Maybe the fresh morning air would clear his head the rest of the way, Alex mused as he carried his cup through the living room toward the front door. Obviously he was still a bit rattled, since he hadn't been acting quite like himself ever since Carly Fletcher had brought him home with her. It really was a beautiful morning, Alex noted when he walked outside with his coffee. Fall hadn't yet fully arrived in this part of the country, but he would bet the hills would be beautiful when it did. Too bad he wouldn't be here to see it.

He sat on a big oak rocker on the front porch, drinking his coffee and filling his lungs with fresh country air. A nice change from processed, sterilized hospital air, he mused.

A high-pitched sound from across the road caught his attention. He noted that the big, sliding door to the workshop behind the house was open and that the sound seemed to be coming from there. A power saw of some sort? Having little experience with tools designed to cut anything other than human bodies, Alex couldn't immediately identify the source of the noise.

A dog barked, and Alex turned his attention to the side yard of the house opposite, where a half-grown pup raced up and down the length of a chain-link fence. A friendly mutt, he seemed to be calling Alex over to play. Alex grinned and lifted his coffee mug in greeting.

The pup yapped again, wagging his entire back end, and began to dig energetically at what appeared to be a depression in the ground next to the fence. Alex frowned. The dog seemed intent on digging his way out of the fenced yard. Minutes later, he succeeded. With a yelp of victory, the dog squirmed through the narrow opening beneath the fence, emerged on the other side and dashed toward the porch where Alex sat, heedless of possible danger from the road he had to cross on the way.

Alex set his empty coffee mug on the porch, stood,

then bent to catch the dog as he pelted toward him. The dog, which seemed to be mostly beagle with a few other breeds mixed in, frantically panted and wiggled and tried to taste Alex's face with an eager tongue.

"Yuck," Alex muttered when the dog narrowly missed licking him right on the mouth. "Calm down, will you, mutt? And stop acting so proud of yourself. Digging out of your yard is not a good thing."

The dog grinned and slobbered on Alex's shirt. Alex gathered the mutt in his arms and stood. "I'd better get you home before you get lost or run over."

The dog didn't try to resist being carried back home.

Following the noises coming from the workshop, Alex stepped to the open doorway. "Hello?"

Inside the well-supplied shop, a lanky-limbed man was bent over a table saw, carefully running a length of board along the blade. He wore a denim shirt with the sleeves rolled up, blue jeans and work boots. His clothing and his thick mop of brown hair were sprinkled with sawdust. His ears were covered by heavy, red plastic hearing protectors, and safety goggles covered the upper half of his face. There was no way he'd heard Alex's greeting.

The dog barked and squirmed. Alex held on tightly, waiting for a chance to safely catch the owner's attention. To his relief, the guy turned off the saw only moments later. The sudden silence in the shop was almost startling. The dog barked again.

The man turned, spotted Alex in the doorway and straightened in surprise. He tugged off the hearing protectors and goggles, revealing a tanned face and friendly brown eyes. Alex guessed him to be somewhat younger than he was—midthirties, perhaps.

"Why, hello."

At the sound of his master's voice, the dog wriggled more energetically, nearly causing Alex to drop him.

"I was sitting on the porch across the road when your dog dug a hole under your fence," Alex explained. "I was afraid he might be hit by a car."

The other man reached out to take the dog. "Thanks. I appreciate your concern." Looking into the dog's adoring eyes, the owner frowned and scolded, "Bad boy, Francis. Have you forgotten everything I told you last time you dug your way out?"

"Francis?" Alex couldn't help grinning. It seemed like such an oddly formal name for the goofy-looking dog.

The man smiled in return. "Seemed like a good idea at the time." Tucking the dog football-fashion beneath his left arm, he extended his right hand. "I'm Bob Calhoun. You must be Carly's brother Mike. I've already met the other two brothers."

Alex found himself oddly taken aback at being mistaken for Carly's brother. The thoughts he'd had of the attractive doctor since he'd met her had been far from fraternal.

"I'm Alex Keating," he corrected. "One of Carly's patients, actually," he added, motioning toward the dark purple bruise at his temple.

"She's brought home another one, has she?" Bob Calhoun chuckled indulgently, not seeming in the least surprised. "That's our Carly."

There were several things about Bob's comments that bothered Alex. The suggestion that she made a habit of bringing home strangers, for one, when Alex had rather fancied the idea that she'd made an exception for him. And the way Bob had referred to her as "our Carly." Did this guy have something going on with the pretty doctor? And why should Alex mind so much if he did?

"You new in the area, Alex?"

"Just visiting. I'm staying in one of the fishing cabins on the river. That's why Carly insisted on bringing me home. She diagnosed a possible concussion and refused to let me go back to the cabin alone."

"Sounds just like her. Did Betty stuff you with food?"

Alex smiled faintly. "Yes."

"She's a great cook, isn't she? She's fed me quite a few times since I moved here. She seems to think a bachelor can't fend for himself.... And who am I to argue with her if it gets me home-cooked meals several times a month?"

Maybe the guy *was* seeing Carly, Alex mused. They were both single, after all. And Betty obviously liked Bob, if she went to the trouble of cooking for him so often.

He hoped they would all be very happy together, Alex thought glumly.

Wanting a distraction from the direction his thoughts had taken, he nodded toward the wood stacked at Bob's feet. "What are you making?"

"An entertainment center. It's a commissioned piece, customized to fit into a narrow space."

"What wood are you using? Mahogany?"

"Cherry," Bob corrected. "You do any woodworking, Alex?"

Alex shook his head. ''Never had an opportunity to try it.''

Bob patted his table saw with his free hand. ''There's nothing like the satisfaction of building something out of a stack of wood and some good power tools.''

Alex's smile deepened. ''You sound a bit like that guy on TV. The one who grunts every time he sees a power tool.''

''At least I don't end up in the emergency room every time I turn one on,'' Bob replied with a chuckle.

Ruefully, Alex touched his bandage again. ''You've got the advantage over me, then. I was just fishing when this happened.''

Bob laughed. Francis, who'd grown impatient at being held for so long, yapped and began to wiggle more furiously to be let down. ''I'd better go take care of that hole,'' Bob remarked. ''Nice to meet you, Alex. Stop by again sometime while you're in the area and I'll let you play with a sander or something.''

Alex chuckled. Damned if he didn't like the guy, despite his possible involvement with Carly Fletcher—though why that should make any difference, Alex didn't even want to consider.

''What's this I hear about you taking a strange man home with you last night?'' Debbie McElroy, L.P.N., planted her hands on her skinny hips as she asked Carly the question, both disapproval and curiosity in her typically stern expression.

Her left hand still resting on the telephone she had just hung up, Carly sighed and pushed her right hand through her limp-feeling hair. She hadn't had time to style it that morning, had barely had time to brush it as she dashed out of her house in response to an emergency call. She'd just made arrangements for Mr. White to be transferred from the small local medical facility to a large teaching hospital in Little Rock. The staff there would be better qualified to treat his life-threatening condition.

She had hardly had a chance to think about Alex Keating since she'd left him sleeping at her house. But now the nurse's question brought his image very clearly into her mind again. His dark good looks. His piercing blue eyes. The slight smile that had made an odd shiver run through her. The way he'd looked, lying tousled and sleepy-eyed against the pillows of her guest bed.

Carly tried to hide her disconcerting reactions behind a shield of dry humor. "He can't help being strange," she quipped. "He's from Boston."

Debbie didn't smile. "Who is he? What's he doing here? What in the world were you thinking when you took him home with you?"

"His name is Alex Keating, he's here on vacation, and I was thinking that he needed someone to check on him during the night. He fell while fishing and knocked himself out. Had Burle and Jeff not been fishing right around the bend from him, close enough to hear a shout and a splash, he might well have drowned."

"But you don't know him. And you took him into your home without a thought?"

"He's very nice," Carly answered rather lamely.

"At least tell me you didn't leave him alone in the house with your grandmother."

"I—er—"

Debbie's eyes widened. "You did! Carly, have you lost your mind?"

"My grandmother is perfectly safe. I'm not an idiot, Debbie, don't treat me like one."

"For a doctor, you are very naive," Debbie grumbled. "Don't you ever watch TV? You can't just be taking strangers into your house. Especially strangers from Boston."

"You make it sound as though Boston were populated by criminals."

"You never heard of the Boston strangler?"

Carly had to laugh at that. "Honestly, Debbie. Why are you always such a pessimist?"

"I happen to think I'm a realist," the nurse retorted.

Carly shook her head in defeat. "I'm too tired to argue with you now, Deb. I've got about an hour before my next appointment, which just barely gives me time to get home, take my guest back to his fishing cabin and get back here. Hold down the fort while I'm gone, will you?"

"You know I will."

"I know." Carly smiled. "That's why I keep you around, despite your gloomy disposition."

Debbie's frown only deepened. "I just hope your grandmother is all right when you get home," she said dolefully.

Alex was crossing the road from Bob's house when Carly climbed out of her truck in her driveway. She waved to Bob, who was kneeling by the hole beneath his fence while Francis romped around him.

"Did Francis dig out again?" she called.

"Yeah," Bob called back. "Your guest very kindly returned the stupid dog to me."

"That dog's not so stupid," Alex commented, reaching Carly's side. "He got out of that fence fast enough when he wanted."

Carly looked up at Alex, searching his face with a concern in her chocolate eyes that he assumed was merely professional. "How are you?" she asked. "Any dizziness? Nausea? Loss of appetite?"

"No dizziness. No nausea. And your grandmother can testify that my appetite is fine. You have beautiful eyes."

The abrupt compliment left him before he was even aware of thinking it. He wasn't sure why he said it.... Maybe because he was tired of pretty Carly Fletcher seeing only a list of potential symptoms when she looked at him. Or maybe he wanted to make sure he was the only man she was thinking about at the moment.

If his subconscious plan had been to draw her attention away from her friendly neighbor, he seemed to have succeeded. Carly stared at him, apparently caught completely off guard by his words.

"I—er—thank you," she said after a moment, then hid once again behind brusque professionalism. "If you think you'll need any pain medication for today, I can write a prescription. There's a pharmacy on the way back to your cabin."

He shook his head. "No need. If I get a headache, I'll take an over-the-counter medication. How did your emergency call work out this morning?"

Again, she seemed a bit startled by the change of topic, but she replied more easily this time. "I've transferred my patient to Little Rock. He's been moved to the top of the list for a kidney transplant."

Alex might have asked a few more specific questions about the man's condition, but he still wasn't ready to talk medicine with Carly. He was no more eager for her to view him as a colleague than as another patient. He wanted Carly to see him as a man—preferably one that she found attractive.

Why that was becoming more important to him every minute, he couldn't quite explain, even to himself. It usually didn't matter to him what anyone thought of him. But then, the women who interested him rarely showed so little interest in return.

He'd gotten spoiled, he thought wryly. Apparently his career success—and maybe his recent mention in *Prominence Magazine*—had gone to his head.

Carly glanced at her watch. "I have to get back to the clinic. Would you like me to drive you to your cabin first, or would you like to rest here awhile longer? You're welcome to stay as long as you like."

"Thank you, but I'll go on back to the cabin. I have some fish to catch."

Her left eyebrow shot up and she looked pointedly at the bruise on his head. She didn't say anything, but she didn't have to.

Alex chuckled. "I'll use my fishing rod this time."

"Good choice. I'm not sure your head can take another confrontation with a rock."

Her smile, Alex realized in wonder, transformed her face from merely pretty to downright breathtaking. He had to make an effort to recover enough breath to say, "I'll, er, I'll get my bag."

"I'll check in with my grandmother while you're getting your things together."

Alex nodded, turned and walked toward the house. It was definitely time he went back to the cabin, he told himself. He'd come to Arkansas to pursue rest, peace and fish, in that order. Not the local doctor.

Carly had to step into the restroom to splash cool water on her face before she went in search of her grandmother. For some reason, she was unusually warm—and had been ever since Alex Keating had gazed into her eyes and told her they were beautiful. And then, only moments later, he'd looked at her smile with a gleam of hunger that had only intensified the heat building inside her.

What on earth had happened out there? Or had she only imagined that something had?

It was a good thing Alex was leaving her home today, she thought, fanning her still-flushed face with one hand. She had no intention of falling for the pretty face and smooth flattery of a man who would only be in town for another few days—even if her heart *had* fluttered in her chest when he smiled at her and told her she had beautiful eyes.

On impulse, Alex kissed Betty's cheek after thanking her for feeding him and taking him in for the evening. The gesture seemed to please her; she blushed rosily and patted his arm.

"You'll come back for dinner tomorrow evening," she said, making the offer sound more like a royal summons than an invitation. "We're having a few friends over, and there will be plenty of food for one more."

Taken off guard, Alex hesitated a moment.

"Alex didn't intend to spend his entire vacation

with us, Granny,'' Carly said quickly. ''He might have other plans for tomorrow evening.''

Alex wasn't sure if she was giving him a graceful way out or making excuses to keep him away.

It was that last possibility that made him lift his chin, flash his most winning smile and say, ''Thank you, Betty. I'd love to join you for dinner tomorrow.''

He was watching Carly's face out of the corner of his eye as he spoke. Whatever emotions she felt at his acceptance, she managed to keep them hidden behind a polite half smile.

Betty made no attempt to hide her own satisfaction. She nodded. ''Good. We'll see you at seven, then.''

''I'll be here,'' he replied. It was a promise to Betty. But for some inexplicable reason, he also felt as if he'd just issued a challenge to Carly.

Three

Carly seemed to be in such a hurry to get rid of him that Alex wouldn't have been entirely surprised had she just slowed in front of his cabin and advised him to jump from the moving truck. But she came to a full stop in the driveway beside his rented car and looked at him with a polite smile. "Is there anything else you need before I go?"

His keys in his hand, Alex considered her question for a moment. He wondered what she would say if he answered honestly. If he told her that he needed to know why she intrigued him so much, why he had become obsessed with the idea of kissing her, discovering just what lay behind that professional doctor's facade of hers. He needed to find out if this was only a temporary aberration, brought on by proximity, circumstance and perhaps a minor head injury...or if there was something more to it.

Since he knew without doubt that he would be seeing more of Dr. Carly Fletcher before he left the area, he only shook his head and said, "No, not just now. Thanks for everything."

She nodded. "You seem to be recovering quite nicely, but don't hesitate to call or come by the clinic if you develop any problems with nausea, dizziness or double vision."

"Right. So...I'll see you at dinner tomorrow evening."

She moistened her lips. "Um...I know Granny put you on the spot with the invitation. If there are other ways you'd rather spend your vacation than having dinner with us, she'll understand."

Again, Alex suspected that Carly was trying to discourage him from spending more time with her. And he couldn't help wondering why. Though he wasn't so sure it was such a good idea himself, innate pride and stubbornness made him smile blandly and say, "I wouldn't miss it for the world."

To Carly's credit, her polite expression didn't change. "Fine. We'll see you then. Good day, Mr. Keating."

Her sudden return to formality amused him. "Good day, Dr. Fletcher," he replied, his tone openly mocking.

She flushed and started the engine. Alex decided he'd better make his exit quickly...before she decided she *should* push him out of her moving vehicle.

Something about that man irritated her. Carly couldn't say what it was exactly. He was polite enough. He'd been very gracious to her grandmother. He'd even returned Bob's runaway puppy. And yet he looked at Carly with the most annoying hint of secret amusement in his dark blue eyes...and something else, something deeper that she didn't want to examine too closely. Something that elicited a response she didn't want to try to interpret, either.

Funny, she had never considered herself a coward. But every time she looked at Alex Keating, mental alarm bells went off inside her head, urging her to run for safety. She couldn't explain it. Didn't particularly like it. But she had to acknowledge it.

He disturbed her almost as much as he irritated her.

Maybe it had something to do with the attraction she felt every time she looked at him. The feminine curiosity that plagued her when she looked at his firm mouth and imagined it pressed against hers, or wondered how his strong arms would feel locked around her.

It had been a long time since Carly had reacted so intensely to anyone. She'd been badly hurt the last time she'd fallen for a man—who, as it turned out, hadn't been what he'd seemed. She didn't want to put herself in that position again with someone who was only passing through.

And wasn't it ridiculous of her to even be thinking along those lines about a man she'd known less than twenty-four hours? A man who'd done nothing more to express interest in her than mention that she had nice eyes. Beautiful eyes, actually, she corrected herself with another disturbing shiver of pleasure at the memory.

"Carly? Dr. Fletcher!"

Carly blinked and started, realizing that her name must have been spoken several times before her attention had finally been claimed. She looked at the doorway of her office, where Debbie McElroy stood frowning at her.

"I'm sorry, Debbie. I was...thinking about a patient," Carly said a bit sheepishly. It wasn't exactly a lie. Alex had been brought to her as a patient. And she'd managed to think of him that way for the most part...until he'd made that comment about her eyes.

"Humph." Debbie looked at her a bit suspiciously

for a moment, then shrugged. "Mrs. Coopersmith is waiting for you in room two. Here's her file."

"Thanks, Debbie." Determined that Alex Keating was not going to interfere with her routine any more than he already had that day, Carly made an attempt to put him out of her mind as she took the file, tossed her hair out of her face and went to deal with Mrs. Coopersmith's chronic gastritis.

By the time the next evening rolled around, Alex wasn't so sure that having dinner with Carly and Betty Fletcher was such a great idea, after all.

He'd had a pretty good two days. Spent some time sitting outside the cabin, reading and watching squirrels romp through the treetops. A couple of deer had wandered close to the edge of the woods, pausing long enough for Alex to admire them before they disappeared into the brush. The frozen dinner he'd nuked for lunch earlier had been surprisingly tasty, containing ingredients that had closely resembled real food.

He'd only thought about Carly Fletcher a dozen times or so. Why risk sitting across a table from her again? Getting all worked up over her beautiful brown eyes. Watching for the flash of smile that turned her face from ordinarily pretty to extraordinarily desirable. Wondering what the odds were that before his vacation ended, he would get to know Carly Fletcher a great deal more intimately.

He should stay right where he was. Fish. Read. Rest. Watch the wildlife. Exactly what he'd planned on doing when he left Boston without even thinking about asking anyone to come along with him. There'd been a couple of women who probably would have accepted, had he asked, but he hadn't, because he didn't want to spend his precious vacation time with either one of them. And now he found himself trying to think of ways to spend more of it with Carly Fletcher.

All this fresh air and free time must be going to his injured head.

Still, at the appointed time, he drove his rented car into the driveway of the yellow frame house and parked beside a practical red hatchback. He looked at it glumly, wondering if it belonged to yet another of Carly's admirers.

What the hell was he doing here, anyway?

Betty answered the door in response to his buzz. She beamed up at him, apparently delighted to see him. "You look much better," she exclaimed. "The color's back in your face and those pretty blue eyes of yours are sparkling. I'm glad to see it."

Alex hadn't blushed since…well, ever. But he felt his cheeks go suspiciously warm in response to Betty's comments. He'd deliberately commented on Carly's eyes to disconcert her yesterday; he wasn't accustomed to having the tables turned so neatly on himself, even inadvertently.

"Er…thanks," he muttered, not knowing what else to say.

Suddenly remembering the bouquet of flowers he'd impulsively purchased at a little florist shop he'd passed on the way, he held them out to her. "These are for you," he said, not quite as smooth as he usually was when making such gestures.

Betty carried on over the flowers as if they'd been dipped in gold. "They're so lovely! What a sweet gesture," she exclaimed. And then she rose on tiptoe to brush her lips across Alex's cheek, which only made him blush again, to his chagrin. Apparently, he had an unexpected susceptibility to both of the Fletcher women.

Betty ushered Alex into the living room. His attention went immediately to Carly. She was dressed for comfort in a heather-plaid cotton shirt and navy chinos, but from the way Alex reacted to her, she might as well have been wearing sequins and diamonds.

He wished he understood what it was about this particular woman that appealed to him so strongly. She was so different from the women he'd been in the habit of dating lately. But then, he hadn't been interested enough in any of those women to even consider asking one of them to share his bed, much less his vacation, with him, he reminded himself.

"Good evening, Doctor," he said, holding her gaze with his.

"Good evening," she replied, neither her expression nor her tone giving a clue to her feelings.

"Hey, Alex. Good to see you again."

Alex turned to nod at Bob Calhoun. Carly's affable neighbor—was that all he was to her?—stuck out his right hand with a friendly smile. "How's the head?"

"Better, thanks." Alex shook Bob's hand. "How's Francis?"

"Tried to dig out again this morning, the dumb mutt. But I've buried chicken wire around the perimeters of the fence. I think that'll hold him."

"Alex, I'd like you to meet our other guest," Betty said, placing her hand on the arm of a skinny, thirty-something redhead who was looking at Alex with a hint of suspicion. "This is Debbie McElroy, Carly's nurse at the clinic. Debbie, our new friend, Alex Keating."

"It's nice to meet you, Ms. McElroy."

She inclined her head a fraction of an inch. Her mop of copper curls swayed slightly around her pale oval face with the movement. Alex thought she wouldn't be half bad-looking if she'd smile, but that didn't appear to be something she was inclined to do when she looked at him.

"I'd already left the clinic when you were brought in the other night. I hear you're from Boston."

Something in her tone made being from Boston sound like a crime. Alex felt almost as if he should apologize to her. "Yes," he said instead. "I'm from Boston."

"Humph. You're a long way from home, Mr. Keating."

"I'm visiting your area on vacation. It certainly lives up to every nice thing my travel agent said about it."

The nurse wasn't easily mollified. She merely nodded again, as if acknowledging the indisputable facts in his statement, then turned away.

"She's really a dear girl," Betty murmured for Alex's hearing alone. "Just a little slow to warm up to strangers."

Alex couldn't help chuckling at that, but he managed to mask it with a slight cough. Slow to warm up? Nurse Debbie had done everything but hold up a cross at him. Alex didn't know if she regarded all strangers that way or if, for some reason, that privilege had been reserved for him alone. Nor did he care, really. He was an old hand at mingling politely at dinner parties; it was something he'd been forced to do regularly in the course of his career.

The conversation during dinner was illuminating.

Long before the delicious food had disappeared, Alex decided that Bob Calhoun wouldn't be competition for Carly's attentions. Bob, Alex concluded, was head over heels in love with Debbie McElroy. How the grumpy nurse felt about Bob was anyone's guess.

"So, what time are we meeting in the morning?" Debbie asked as she plowed through her dinner with an incredibly hearty appetite for someone so thin. Her question seemed to be directed at Bob and Carly jointly.

Bob glanced questioningly at Carly.

"Seven?" Carly suggested.

Debbie groaned. "Seven? On Saturday? My only day to sleep late?"

"It's an hour and a half drive, Deb," Bob reminded her. "If we start any later, we won't have enough time."

She sighed deeply. "All right. Fine. Seven. Maybe I can catch a nap in the car on the way. Assuming you drive more sensibly than you usually do, of course," she added with a pointed look across the table at Bob.

Bob lifted both eyebrows. "I always drive sensibly."

"It's a wonder you haven't killed me already," she muttered. "Every time I get in your car I say a prayer."

"Of gratitude, no doubt," Bob replied without missing a beat.

Debbie snorted. And Alex would have sworn he saw a fleeting gleam of hunger in Bob's dark eyes before the other man swiftly masked the expression and turned to Alex. "You ever do any caving, Alex?"

Alex was surprised at the sudden change of topic. "Caving? As in climbing down into them?"

"Yes. There are a lot of caves and caverns in north Arkansas and southern Missouri. Debbie and Carly and I are going into a cavern in Missouri tomorrow."

Alex glanced at Carly, trying to imagine her mucking through a cave. "This is something you enjoy?" he asked her.

She smiled in response to his dubious tone. "Very much."

Climbing through caves sounded like something that would appeal to kids, perhaps, but hardly to a group of adults that included a doctor, a nurse and a carpenter. "Why?" he asked blankly.

She laughed. "It's fun. Sometimes we survey and map the caverns we explore, other times we keep a log of the cave life we find. Tomorrow we're just going to work our way through to keep in shape. Caving is a physically demanding hobby."

"Why don't you go with us, Alex?" Bob asked.

Both Carly and Debbie looked startled by Bob's impulsive invitation—Alex wasn't sure which of them was most dismayed by the possibility of his inclusion on their outing. The sensible thing to do of course—both for their sake and his own—would be to decline immediately. He'd never been caving in his life, and he was perfectly content to keep it that way. And yet...

Still looking at Carly, he said, "It sounds intriguing."

Betty looked delighted by the idea. "You should go with them, Alex. It will be something to talk about when you go home from your vacation. Something you've never done before. I think you'd have a lovely time.''

As if prodded by her grandmother's enthusiasm, Carly nodded. ''We'd be delighted to have you join us, Alex. Wouldn't we, Debbie?''

Debbie frowned. ''He's never been caving before. He doesn't even have any equipment.''

''I have duplicates of everything,'' Bob assured them. ''Plenty to share with Alex.''

Alex looked at Bob. ''What equipment would I need?''

''A good pair of hiking boots with gripping soles. I have an extra pair—as long as you wear a size ten.''

''I'm an eleven,'' Alex replied. ''But I have hiking boots.''

''They'll get wet and muddy,'' Bob warned.

''It wouldn't be the first time. What else?''

This time it was Carly who answered. ''Warm, sturdy clothes. Several layers. The temperature in the cave is between fifty and fifty-six degrees, and the humidity close to one hundred percent. And they should be old clothes that you wouldn't mind ruining. Cave mud doesn't always wash out without staining.''

''Gloves are a must,'' Bob added. ''I've got several pairs of good gloves, so don't worry about that. I've got an extra helmet with a headlamp, too, but everyone carries at least two extra light sources. You have a flashlight or two with you?''

Alex nodded. He'd packed several flashlights, just in case there was a loss of electricity in his isolated fishing cabin. ''Anything else?''

''Knee pads,'' Debbie replied. ''You'll be crawling over some hard, rocky places, through openings barely big enough to squeeze through. Sure you're up to that so soon after your accident?'' Her voice held just a hint of challenge.

''Yes, I'll be fine.'' It was all Alex could do to answer civilly. Debbie's attitude was beginning to irk him. If a nurse on *his* staff talked to him that way, he'd...

But she wasn't on his staff, he reminded himself. She didn't know he was a doctor and probably wouldn't treat him any differently if she did. He was just going to have to get used to her if he planned to spend time with her in a cave—and apparently he was planning just that. He wasn't sure exactly when he'd decided to go along, but he knew why he had.

He wanted to spend more time with Carly.

Debbie didn't look reassured. ''You slipped and fell while fishing. This isn't a commercial cave, with neatly laid-out paths and guardrails. This is a wild cave, with uneven floors and narrow passages and some sheer drops that can be dangerous if you aren't very careful.''

Now Alex *was* annoyed. ''Despite first impressions, I'm not a klutz,'' he said firmly. ''I've been rock climbing as a hobby for several years, and that isn't a picnic, either. I'm quite sure I can handle caving.''

''What about claustrophobia? We'll be squeezing into places barely wide enough for your shoulders. Wouldn't want you to get in there and have a panic attack. You're too big for us to carry out.''

Alex set his teeth. ''I am not claustrophobic. And I do not have panic attacks.''

''So you'll join us? Great,'' Bob enthused, without giving Alex time to answer. ''It'll be nice to have another guy along. I'm usually sadly outnumbered.''

Just to be perverse, Alex slid easily back into the charm that came so naturally to him when he chose to utilize it. "I'm surprised you want me along," he said to Bob. "I wouldn't blame you for wanting to keep these two pretty ladies all to yourself."

Carly blushed. Debbie scowled. Betty giggled.

Bob laughed out loud. "This is going to be fun," he predicted.

Alex knew he wasn't the only one at the table who wondered if Bob was being overly optimistic.

"I'm sure you'll all have a wonderful time," Betty said firmly. "Now, is everyone ready for dessert?"

They all looked down at their empty plates.

"I'm *always* ready for dessert," Bob announced.

Betty disappeared into the kitchen. She returned carrying an enormous chocolate cake on which flickered perhaps a dozen multicolored candles. "The day before yesterday was Alex's birthday," she said with a smile for him. "I thought he should have something to remember about the occasion other than a bump on the head."

She set the cake in front of him and began to sing, "Happy birthday to you..." The others quickly joined in with more enthusiasm than harmony. Rather embarrassed—and unexpectedly touched—Alex suffered through it with a forced smile.

He hadn't expected to get involved with this bunch when he'd headed off for his solitary vacation in rural Arkansas. And he wasn't sure now whether he was pleased or dismayed that he had.

Carly was thinking half-seriously of strangling Bob Calhoun. As good and dear a man as he was, he definitely deserved throttling after what he'd done tonight. How could he have invited Alex Keating to go on their caving expedition with them?

While the others finished their dessert, Carly toyed with her own, reminding herself that Bob had only been generous and hospitable by asking a visitor to their area to join them for some local entertainment. He couldn't have known that Alex would accept, and he couldn't have realized how Carly would react to that acceptance.

How could Bob have known that the idea of spending hours in a dark, narrow cave with Alex Keating would make Carly break into a sweat of sheer panic, mixed with a healthy dose of lust?

She couldn't understand herself what was happening to her where this man was concerned. She'd never thought she would react so strongly to a gorgeous face. Dark, thick hair. Piercing, navy blue eyes. Chiseled features, a slightly dimpled chin and a sexier-than-all-get-out mouth. Six feet plus of sheer male perfection. Was she really shallow enough to fall for that delectable outward appearance?

Apparently, she was.

But she was honest enough to admit to herself that it wasn't only Alex's looks she found appealing. She liked his smile. His kindness to her grandmother. The dry wit he occasionally revealed. The way his eyes gleamed when he looked at her, making her feel almost beautiful...and much more interesting than a simple country doctor.

She seemed to have a talent for being attracted to the wrong men. She'd been devastated to discover that the first man she thought she loved didn't even exist. She didn't even like the man she'd discovered when he'd finally revealed his true self to her. Linc

Saunders had seemed so straight and genuine, so honest and noble. But once she'd gotten to know him, she'd learned that he was anything but honest, noble or genuine.

For all she knew, Alex Keating was just like Linc—charming and nice on the outside, devious and selfish on the inside.

"You remember that, don't you, Carly?" Bob asked. He'd been entertaining Alex with tales of their caving misadventures.

She blinked, caught Alex's gaze and realized that he was aware that she had no idea what had been said. The gleam of amusement in his eyes almost made her squirm. Could he possibly have guessed that she'd been thinking about him?

"Um, yes, of course," she said, then quickly changed the subject, blurting out the first thing that popped into her head. "What time did we say we're leaving in the morning?"

"Seven," Alex reminded her before the others could speak. "Are we meeting here?"

"My place," Bob corrected. "We'll take my four-wheel drive."

Debbie glanced at her watch. "I'd better head home soon if I'm going to have everything ready in the morning."

"Me, too," Bob agreed. "I'll have a pack ready for you, Alex."

"Thank you."

"No problem."

Carly subsided again into thoughts of doing bodily harm to her overly gracious neighbor.

Bob and Debbie stayed only long enough after dinner to help clear away the dishes. Both thanked Betty profusely for the meal before they left. Alex noted that even Debbie was notably warmer toward Betty than she seemed to be to anyone else. He also noticed that Debbie seemed to avoid touching Bob as they walked side by side out the front door.

Apparently, Bob's infatuation was not reciprocated. Poor guy. Alex had always been very careful not to make a lovesick fool of himself over any woman. He had no intention of beginning now, he reminded himself with a sideways glance at Carly.

It didn't help his confidence that just looking at her as she smiled and waved goodbye to her other guests caused a renewed wave of heat to spill through him. He felt a fierce hunger to have her turn that smile his way. But when she looked at him, the smile vanished, replaced by the cautious expression she seemed always to wear for him.

"Can I get you anything else, Alex?" Betty asked as the three of them lingered in the living room.

He smiled at her. "No, thank you, Betty. I should be on my way."

"Drive carefully, dear. Those roads out by the river are terrible."

"I'm getting used to them. Thank you again for dinner. It was delicious. The best meal I've had in a long time."

"You're quite welcome. It was a pleasure to have you join us. Carly, walk Alex to his car. I'm just going to finish a few things in the kitchen and then I'll be turning in."

"It really isn't necessary for you to walk me to my car," Alex murmured to Carly when her grandmother had disappeared into the other room. "I'm quite capable of making that trip on my own."

Her lips curved into a very faint smile and she shook her head. ''I have to,'' she explained, and reached for the door. ''My grandmother told me to.''

Alex followed her outside. ''Are you always so obedient?''

''Of course. Haven't you realized by now that my grandmother is a real tyrant? Whatever it takes, she's going to have her way.''

Closing the front door behind them, Alex chuckled. ''I find that hard to believe. She seems to be a gentle, sweet, perfectly harmless lady.''

''Boy, has she got you fooled. Behind that sweet-little-old-lady smile lies the soul of a Hun.''

Alex laughed. ''That's terrible.''

''But true. I love her dearly, but I've been known to shake in my boots at the thought of defying her.''

Betty sounded like a good ally to have. Alex wondered half-seriously how she would react if he told her that he was thinking about having a hot and heavy vacation affair with her granddaughter—and asked her to consider ordering Carly to cooperate.

Carly patted the hood of Alex's rental car. ''Well, here you are. Delivered safe and sound to your vehicle. Now my grandmother can rest easily.''

''Thank you for the escort,'' he said, gravely inclining his head. ''I'm not sure I could have made it without you.''

Carly laughed, her white teeth flashing in the shadows cast by the overhead security light. ''You're quite welcome, sir.''

Perhaps he could have behaved himself if she hadn't laughed. The sweet, musical sound was still echoing in his head when he reached out to her, placing his hands on her shoulders and drawing her slowly toward him. He gave her plenty of time to resist, but she didn't. Maybe she was simply too surprised to react.

He brushed his lips over hers, then kissed her again. He somehow managed to keep the embrace light, nonthreatening, when what he really wanted was to crush her mouth beneath his, to slide his tongue between her lips and plunge deeply inside to taste her. He kept his hands on her shoulders, resisting an almost overwhelming urge to slide them lower, to explore her slender curves, to fill his palms with the soft breasts brushing lightly against his chest as he stood so close to her.

He didn't linger long enough to press his luck. He drew back reluctantly, pausing only long enough to say, "I've been wanting to do that ever since you patched me up and brought me home with you."

Her eyes were huge, her kiss-dampened mouth rounded in surprise. Very quickly, she retreated behind that professional primness he'd seen her utilize before. "I think you should know," she said, her voice only slightly husky, "I don't get romantically entangled with my patients."

He found her wording rather amusing, though he had no inclination to laugh. He looked at her without smiling. "I'm not one of your patients."

"I..."

"I didn't come here looking for 'romantic entanglements,'" he continued quietly, adding a touch of irony to the words. "Just the opposite, in fact. I wanted to be alone."

She winced. "You, um, haven't been alone much since you fell and were brought to me."

"No. But I'm not complaining."

She twisted her hands in front of her. "Alex, I..."

Again, her voice faded, leaving the sentence unfinished.

"Why do I make you so nervous?" he asked. He saw immediate denial in the lift of her chin, the crease of her brow. And then she glanced down at her hands, which were still clasped so tightly in front of her that he could see her knuckles gleaming white in the shadows.

"I don't know," she finally said.

He thought about that for a moment. Could it be that Carly was as taken aback by the attraction between them as he was? Or was he only hoping that she was feeling the same things he was?

He touched her cheek, letting his fingertips linger at the corner of her mouth. "Don't be afraid of me," he murmured. "I'm not dangerous."

"I'm not afraid of you," she corrected him quickly. Then added after a brief hesitation, "But you do make me nervous."

His sudden smile surprised them both. "I think I like that."

And then he brushed her mouth with his one more time before he made himself open his car door, climb inside and start the engine.

He was aware that Carly didn't immediately go inside but stood watching him back out of the driveway. He would have given a great deal of money to know what she was thinking as he drove away.

Four

Not dangerous? Hah! Alex Keating could be the most dangerous man Carly had encountered in a very long time.

She'd come to that conclusion sometime during a long, restless night. She should have been sleeping, resting for the strenuous caving expedition the following day. But nearly every time she closed her eyes, she felt Alex's mouth on hers again, felt the warmth of his body as he stood so close to her it would only have taken a slight shift of her weight to put her into his arms.

She'd been almost overwhelmingly tempted to close that slight distance between them. And it was her own inclinations, as much as Alex's unexpected kisses, that had her lying awake, staring at her ceiling, wondering what on earth was going on between the two of them. Wondering what she could do to stop it before it got completely out of hand.

Finally giving up on sleep, she got up early. She showered and dressed, trying the entire time to convince herself that this was just a normal caving expedition, no reason to make a big deal out of it. She, Debbie, Bob—and various others—had been doing this sort of thing for a couple of years, exploring many caves in the area, so there was no reason to get all bent out of shape over this trip. She wore a red knit pullover beneath a heavy, red-and-black flannel shirt, faded old jeans and practical, waterproof hiking boots. Hardly seductive attire, she thought in satisfaction as she scraped her hair back into a low ponytail. No one could accuse her of deliberately trying to attract Alex's attentions.

Taking care to be quiet so she wouldn't disturb her grandmother, she ate a bagel and an orange, washing them down with a cup of hot tea. And then she grabbed her pack and headed across the road to Bob's, a full twenty minutes early.

He was already outside, loading supplies into his Blazer.

"Well, good morning," he said, way too cheerful as far as Carly was concerned. "Anxious to get started, are you?"

"I thought I'd see if there's anything I can do to help you," she said airily, hoping her light makeup hid the evidence of her restless night. "Did you find enough duplicate equipment?"

"Yeah, no problem. Alex will be fine."

Just the sound of his name made her shiver. And she would be spending the entire day with him.

She could only hope that more time spent with Alex Keating would lessen her attraction to him, not strengthen it. She wished she could be a bit more optimistic that that would be the case.

"I noticed that Alex didn't stay long after Debbie and I left last night," Bob commented blandly, taking Carly's bag and tossing it into the back of his Blazer with his own stuff. "I was out feeding Francis when you, um, escorted Alex to his car."

Carly felt her cheeks flame. She didn't even want

to think about what Bob had seen or how he'd interpreted the scene. "I..."

"Alex seems like a very nice guy. Of course, it's hard to tell on such short acquaintance. Sometimes people who appear harmless at first turn out to be quite different once you get to know them a little better." Bob's warning was about as subtle as a sledgehammer.

Carly sighed lightly. "I'm thirty-four years old, Bob, and hardly naive. And might I remind you that you're the one who invited Alex to join us today."

His smile was a bit sheepish. "Well, we were breaking a caving rule by only having three in our party rather than the recommended four. Besides, I figured this was a safe way for you to get to know him a little better. His interest in you was obvious during dinner, and I figured he'd be coming back around anyway, so..."

"So you decided to arrange a properly chaperoned outing," Carly cut in sternly. "Honestly, Bob."

"Okay, call me a meddler, but..."

"You're a meddler."

"But," Bob continued doggedly, "you know I only have your best interest at heart."

Carly sighed more deeply. "Yes, I know. But you're off base this time. Even if Alex is the nicest guy in the world, he'll still be going back to Boston in a week or so, and I'm firmly and happily rooted right here. You, of all people, surely aren't advising me to indulge in a vacation affair."

"Hardly," Bob agreed dryly. "But I'm aware that the social opportunities around here are rather limited. I see nothing at all wrong with you enjoying a man's company occasionally. And one never knows how it might turn out."

"You're one to be passing out romantic advice," Carly gibed as Debbie's sensible little Ford turned into Bob's driveway. "Have you made any headway in *your* social life lately?"

"No," Bob admitted. "But it hasn't been for lack of trying," he added as Debbie climbed out of her car. "Good morning, Debbie. Don't you look lovely today."

Since Debbie had dressed as sensibly and grubbily as Carly, she didn't seem to take Bob's words too seriously. "It's much too early for flattery," she grumbled around a yawn. "Where's the pretty boy? Did he wimp out?"

As if on cue, Alex pulled into the driveway.

Promptly at seven, Carly noted with a glance at her watch intended to keep her from staring at Alex as he strode toward them. Yet she'd seen enough to note that Alex did amazing things to a pair of faded jeans and a dark blue chamois-cloth shirt. She shoved her hands into her pockets, trying to ignore a sudden urge to feel the soft brush of chamois against her palms.

When she finally decided she was composed enough to look at him, she found him looking back at her with a slight smile that only made her remember how his lips had felt pressed to hers. She swallowed a groan and managed to speak reasonably coherently. "Good morning, Alex."

"Carly."

Just her name. Funny how different it sounded when he said it. Funny how intensely she reacted to it. She clenched her hands in her pockets and was grateful when he turned to greet Bob and Debbie.

Speaking to Bob, Alex lifted a small duffel bag. "I brought a few things I thought I might need."

Bob nodded and motioned Alex over to the open back of his Blazer. "Just toss it in here. We'll separate everything once we get there. Is everyone ready to go? Anyone need to use the bathroom first?" he asked with a grin, addressing them as if they were schoolchildren.

They all assured him they were fine for the moment.

"I'll ride shotgun," Debbie announced, reaching for the front passenger door with a slightly challenging look at Alex. "I get carsick sometimes on long rides."

Alex simply opened the door behind hers and motioned Carly in. "I'm quite happy to ride in the back seat," he murmured.

Adding Debbie to her to-be-strangled-later list, Carly climbed into the back seat and belted herself in, as close to the opposite door from Alex as physically possible.

Maybe it was only coincidence that Alex seemed to fill almost all the remaining space so that his left thigh occasionally brushed her right one as they got under way. After all, he was long-legged. He probably wasn't intentionally trying to keep her nerve endings buzzing with awareness of him.

Yeah, right, she thought in disbelief as she caught a glimpse of his decidedly wicked half smile.

Bob kept the conversation going during the drive, raising his voice over the country music blaring from his radio to give Alex a series of caving instructions. "Stay close to the team. Watch your head. Be careful where you step—both for your own safety and because of fragile formations and defenseless cave dwellers. And remember the caver's motto—Take only photographs. Leave only carefully placed footprints. Kill only time."

Alex nodded. "I think I can remember all that."

"And keep your gloves on," Debbie added. "This is a living cavern. Still evolving. The oils on your hands are serious pollutants to the ecosystem. You wouldn't believe some of the damage we've seen in local caves. Graffiti. Trash. Beer cans and cigarette butts. Delicate stalactites and stalagmites shattered. It only takes a moment to destroy something that nature took hundreds of years to build."

"There are a lot of caves and caverns in northern Arkansas and southern Missouri," Carly said, feeling as if she should hold up her end of the conversation. "Although 'cave' is the term used most often, a cave is actually one underground room, while caverns are made up of several rooms. Most of the caving injuries I've seen have come from falls. The others are usually from careless mistakes. Cavers who don't wear helmets risk injury from hitting their heads or being hit by falling rock. There's also a danger of flooding after heavy rains. Many cavers have been taken by surprise by flash floods that seemed to come out of nowhere. Some wander off and get lost, leading to a danger of hypothermia and dehydration."

Alex had turned his full attention to Carly as she spoke, shifting in his seat so that his leg brushed hers again. "You make this sound like a dangerous hobby," he said.

The biggest danger she seemed to be in at the moment was melting into a puddle at Alex's feet. Every time he touched her, no matter how seemingly innocently, she warmed another degree or two.

She cleared her throat and spoke primly. "The safety precautions exist for a reason. We try to follow them."

"I notice none of you have used the term spelunkers."

"Most of us prefer cavers, or caving, as opposed to spelunking," Carly explained.

Alex nodded gravely. "I'll keep that in mind. Wouldn't want to sound like an amateur."

"Just remember that you *are* an amateur," Debbie advised curtly. "We don't want to have to haul your butt out of there if you do something dumb."

"Your concern for my welfare is very touching," Alex assured her. "Thank you."

Carly and Bob laughed. Debbie blinked a moment, then broke into a grin. "Just remember what I said, Boston," she muttered with less asperity than before. "Watch yourself today."

Alex looked at Carly with what could only be described as a smug smile. *I'm making progress with Debbie,* his expression seemed to say. *You're next.*

Carly glanced quickly out the window beside her, pretending to take great interest in the passing scenery.

Alex was a bit surprised to discover that Buckman's Caverns were on private land, accessible only by a padlocked gate to which Bob had the combination.

"Mr. Buckman gives out the combination when he accepts a caving group—for a reasonable fee," Bob explained. "When we leave, he'll change the combination. I arranged this outing several weeks ago. He books up to two months in advance—only to groups that he personally approves. I've been here a couple of times before, and he knows I'm careful, but he doesn't let in any group that he suspects will cause damage or carelessly risk injuries."

"I'd like to pay my part of the fee," Alex volunteered.

"Already taken care of this time," Bob assured him. "You're our guest today. Call it a belated birthday present."

These people sure were into birthdays, Alex thought. His own parents hadn't made such a big deal of the occasion. They had simply presented him with his annual check for the maximum amount they could give him without tax penalties—their way of helping him avoid future inheritance taxes—and then wished him a pleasant upcoming year. They hadn't mentioned his birthday again.

Bob closed the gate behind them, then drove down the tree-lined gravel road for perhaps a hundred yards before parking beside a small wooden building.

"Facilities," Debbie said to Alex with a nod of her head toward the unadorned building. "Rough, but adequate. I suggest you make use of them before we start hiking."

"Hiking?" He looked around them, seeing nothing but a well-worn path leading straight into the wooded hills beyond them. "Where is this cavern?"

"An hour's hike away," Debbie replied with a quick, slightly evil grin. "Hope you're in as good a shape as you appear to be, Keating. By the end of the day, you're going to feel every impressive muscle in that gorgeous bod."

Alex saw Bob's eyebrows draw into a slight frown in response to Debbie's outrageous comments. He could have reassured the other man that he needn't take the flattery too seriously. Alex generally knew when a woman was particularly attracted to him. Debbie was not.

Carly, on the other hand...

He shot a sideways glance at her, finding her looking back at him. She looked away quickly, but not before he noted the gleam of awareness in her eyes.

Was he only seeing attraction where he wanted to see it?

While the women made use of the facilities, Bob went to work preparing for the hike. He pulled out two backpacks, one for himself, the other for Alex. He spent the next ten minutes checking the contents and itemizing them for Alex, as well as adding the items Alex had brought.

By the time Alex strapped the pack onto his back, it contained two flashlights; extra batteries and bulbs; a small first-aid kit; a water bottle; two unbreakable plastic baby bottles full of nuts, dried fruits and chocolate pieces—"quick energy for when you start to droop," Bob explained; a large, heavy-duty plastic bag and several smaller ones; a multifunction pocket tool; and a compass. Bob had stuffed knee and elbow pads into the pack, to be donned before they went into the cave; they were too uncomfortable to wear while hiking.

"That should be all you'll need," Bob said, zipping the pack and tossing it to Alex. "I've got a few extra supplies in mine, just in case we need them. Oh, and here's your helmet. No need to wear it until we get to the cave."

The helmet was hard yellow plastic, with an electric light attached to the front and chin straps dangling from beneath. Alex looped a strap of his backpack through a chin strap, letting the helmet dangle behind him.

"Got your gloves?" Debbie asked Alex when they were ready to get under way.

"In my pocket."

Looking thoughtful, Carly gave Alex a visual once-over. "I hope you'll be warm enough," she murmured, motioning vaguely toward his chamois-cloth shirt and jeans.

"I have long underwear beneath this," he assured her. "As a matter of fact, I was just wondering if I've overdressed. I'm *too* warm now."

"You'll be even warmer after hiking for an hour," Debbie commented, seeming to take pleasure in the idea. "Might be fun watching you get all hot and sweaty."

Alex was beginning to understand that Debbie had a very dry, even mischievous, sense of humor, which prompted many of her curmudgeonly comments. And he'd decided the best way to respond to her was in kind.

"Come over to my place tonight and I'll show you hot and sweaty," he shot back at her, cocking his head to a self-confident angle.

She gave a bark of laughter. "In your dreams, Keating."

"We'd better get started," Bob said, his voice uncharacteristically sharp. "Everyone get your stuff and come on."

Alex knew it was no accident that Bob positioned himself very close to Debbie on the narrow path, making sure that Alex stayed farther back with Carly. Which was, of course, just fine with Alex.

"I seem to have stepped on Bob's toes," Alex murmured so that only Carly could hear.

Carly shrugged and kept her face averted as she replied equally softly, "He probably didn't expect you to make a pass at Debbie when he invited you along for today."

Alex couldn't help chuckling at Carly's wording. "I hardly made a pass at her."

Carly glanced at him skeptically. "You invited her to your place to get 'hot and sweaty.' That certainly sounded like a pass to me—or rather, it probably sounded like one to Bob."

"I was only teasing...and Debbie was well aware of it," Alex answered mildly. And then couldn't resist adding, "Sounds to me as if you're jealous—or rather, as if Bob is jealous."

Carly's chin lifted so high she nearly stumbled over a rock in the path. Alex's hand shot out to steady her. She shook him off.

"I can assure you that *I* am not jealous," she whispered heatedly. "As for how Bob feels...that's his business."

"What are you two muttering about back there?" Debbie asked, glancing over her shoulder as she tried to keep up with Bob's brisk strides. "Whatever it is, you're going to get left behind if you don't pick up the pace. Bob seems to think we're running a marathon today."

Obligingly, Bob slowed his steps a bit. Reminding himself that he was the guest today and hadn't intended to cause problems, Alex silently vowed to behave for the remainder of the outing. And then he glanced at Carly, trudging so seriously at his side, her luscious mouth pursed into the slightest of pouts, and he wondered if that was a vow he would be able to keep.

The hike was as long and as strenuous as Alex had been warned to expect. By the end of twenty minutes, he was sweating inside his long underwear and thick socks. Ten minutes later, his hair hung damply around his bruised face, and he'd unfastened the top buttons of his shirt, rolled up the sleeves and pushed up the long sleeves of his undershirt.

He was in danger of evaporating right on the path, he thought grimly, hoping he was hiding his misery from the others. They all seemed to be handling this strenuous trek just fine, despite Debbie's constant complaining. Carly and Debbie had tied their flannel shirts around their waists by the sleeves, leaving them clad only in the thinner pullover tops, while Bob had unbuttoned his own flannel shirt, letting it flap around the knit shirt he wore beneath. They looked warm but more comfortable than Alex.

Alex had prided himself on staying in good shape. Of course, he was a busy man—he didn't have time to get to the health club as often as he might have liked. Hadn't been rock climbing in ages. And it wasn't nearly as warm in Boston at this time of year as it was in Arkansas and Missouri. The list of excuses occupied his mind as he trudged on.

A few minutes later, Bob, who seemed to have become team leader, called for a short rest break. Alex could almost have kissed him. They dropped their packs on the mossy ground. Alex sat on the ground, propped his back against a tree and mopped surreptitiously at his face with one hand. He flinched involuntarily when he brushed against the colorful bruise still decorating his temple.

"Let me see," Carly said immediately, kneeling beside him. That quickly, she'd gone from cool to concerned. The consummate caretaker.

"I'm fine," Alex assured her as her fingertips brushed softly over his skin. "It's just sore."

She lingered a bit longer, studying him closely. He saw the moment when the expression in her eyes changed, when the scrutiny became personal rather than professional. Their gazes locked for a heartbeat...and then Carly quickly backed away.

"You're fine," she said, suspiciously breathless. "It's only a bruise."

"That's what *I* said," he reminded her, tilting the corners of his mouth into a smile. Bob and Debbie, who'd been talking quietly on the other side of the small clearing, picked up their packs.

"Let's go," Bob called out.

Alex was both relieved and surprised when they reached the entrance of the cavern. Relieved because the long hike was over, surprised that the opening was so small. Barely big enough for a man to crawl through, the hole in the side of a rocky hill was covered by a metal grating, secured by another combination padlock.

Bob opened the grating, then turned to Alex while Carly and Debbie donned their flannel shirts, strapped on their helmets and pulled on their knee and elbow pads.

"This is a fairly easy cave," Bob explained. "The entrance is a short drop, less than three feet. There's only one room in which we're likely to get wet, and we won't be doing any vertical caving, which is why I didn't bring rappelling gear. We will, however, be going into some very narrow and low passages, and we'll be passing a few fall-and-dies, so stay alert."

"Fall-and-dies?" Alex lifted an eyebrow as he repeated the phrase that Bob had tossed out so casually. "I suppose that term is self-explanatory?"

The others all nodded.

"We talk about fall-and-dies, fall-and-get-seriously-hurts and fall-and-get-wets," Debbie explained with a grin. "If you can't figure those out, you'd better stay out here in the sunshine where you'll be safe."

Alex only shook his head and struggled into his pads and helmet. The helmet felt heavy and awkward, a bit front-heavy with the light attached over his forehead, but he figured he'd get used to it. The others seemed comfortable enough in theirs.

Bob continued his role as team leader. "I'll go first. Debbie, you follow me, then Alex, then Carly will bring up the rear and assist Alex if necessary."

Carly nodded, apparently resigned to her assignment.

"Any questions before we go in?" Bob asked Alex.

Alex shook his head.

"Let's go, then." Bob lowered himself into the opening and vanished into the darkness within.

Five

Alex had expected to enter one of those huge, gorgeous cavern rooms filled with beautiful formations. He was somewhat disappointed to land on his feet, only to find himself in a tight, low opening just big enough to hold the four of them. It smelled of mud. The walls and ceiling were brown limestone, red-streaked with iron deposits. Even the sunlight filtering through the entrance hole looked brown.

He'd given up a day of his vacation for this, he found himself thinking. He could have been standing in the beautiful river in the sunlight, with a cool breeze blowing on his face, birds serenading him, fish playing tag with his lures. Instead, he was standing in a muddy brown hole. What fun.

And then Carly moved beside him, her breast brushing his arm in the cramped space. He caught a whiff of the faint floral scent he'd already begun to associate with her. And he decided that maybe he'd rather be here in this hole with Carly than in a stream with a fish, after all.

"Through here," Bob said, motioning toward a crack in the far wall that Alex hadn't even noticed. "Turn on your helmet lights and watch your heads."

Alex looked doubtfully at the crack, which hardly looked big enough for scrawny Debbie to get through. But then Bob slipped sideways through the opening and disappeared. Debbie followed easily, and Carly looked promptingly at Alex. "Ready?"

He nodded his helmet-heavy head and turned sideways to wriggle through the crack, which turned out to be longer than he'd expected. It required some effort on his part to work his way through the passage. Carly stayed close behind him, occasionally brushing up against him when he stopped to get his bearings.

The crack widened, then opened at the top of a pile of rocks that Carly called a breakdown—something Alex didn't want to think about too closely. They climbed downward, setting their feet carefully on the moisture-slick rock. And then they were at the bottom, and Alex found the beauty he'd hoped to encounter.

The room they had entered was large, the ceiling a good two stories above their heads. When Alex looked up, the light on his helmet illuminated glistening formations protruding from the ceiling, some thick and solid-looking, others twisted into intriguing shapes, still others so delicate they looked as if a strong breeze would bring them down.

Carly stood beside him, her light aimed with his. "Speleothem," she said, pointing. "Stalactites, helectites, soda straws. On the floor, stalagmites. The colorings come from iron, calcite and phosphates. The formations are caused by water dripping through the rock, leaving clusters of minerals behind on the ceiling or depositing the minerals on the floor below. Very slowly, the mineral deposits continue to build and grow. See those thick columns of rock that go all the way from floor to ceiling? Those are formed over hundreds of years, when stalactites and stalagmites meet and join."

Awed by the magnificence around him, Alex moved slowly around the room, taking care with his steps, studying everything closely. The others watched indulgently, seeming to understand his fascination.

"What do you call this?" he asked, pointing to a part of the wall that looked like flowing lava frozen into place.

"Flowstone," Carly replied with a smile.

"And this?" He pointed his light upward at a wide, rippled formation that looked like pleated curtains.

"They're called draperies, for obvious reasons."

"This is amazing. Who would have dreamed a room this size was hidden beneath the ground?"

"This isn't even a very large room compared to some I've been in," Bob said. "Haven't you ever been through a commercial cave, Alex?"

"Not that I remember, though my parents took me through Carlsbad Caverns when I was a small child. I've seen photographs." Alex stood very close to a massive column, thinking of how many aeons it must have taken to develop. He itched to touch it but was hesitant to do so, even wearing gloves, for fear of making a difference in nature's decorating.

"Your parents aren't into nature outings?" Bob asked.

Alex smiled dryly. "My parents aren't into family outings, period. Their idea of a vacation was to hire a nanny for me while they took off to Europe for a few weeks. The trip to Carlsbad must have been a temporary aberration." He turned away from the column, glanced at the three somber faces looking back at him and shrugged, uncomfortable that he'd answered more revealingly than he'd intended. "Is there more to see?"

"Are you kidding?" Bob said. "We've just gotten started."

For the next hour and a half, they climbed, crawled, duckwalked and wriggled their way into room after room of the cavern system. Through mud, rock piles and bat guano, past the fall-and-die spots Bob had warned of earlier, up walls that barely offered hand- and toeholds, they made their way slowly, carefully, without much conversation. Some passages were deceptive, leading into dead ends or blocked by breakdown piles, others led into a rabbit warren of connecting rooms and openings. Bob remained the leader, being most familiar with this cavern.

Occasionally, one of the others stopped to point out particularly interesting features to Alex in case he missed them on his own. A clump of upside-down bats sleeping crammed together in a tight corner, the huge pile of guano beneath them showing that it was a long-favored spot for the colony. There were other cave dwellers—isopods, cave crickets, assorted creepy-crawlies that didn't seem to bother anyone else but made Alex hope his clothes were all securely fastened around accessible openings.

Bob pointed out a thick stalagmite that looked a bit like two lovers entwined in a passionate embrace, adding that the formation was called—what else?—"the lovers." Carly directed Alex's attention to several clusters of gypsum "flowers," the hydrated calcium and phosphate crystals within them glittering in the beams of their headlamps.

Alex was beginning to understand the attraction of this hobby. As strenuous and uncomfortable as it could be at times—and Bob had told him that this cavern was relatively easy to move through compared to some—there was an innate fascination in climbing through a crack in a wall of rock to discover an underground room filled with impressive natural formations.

They stopped for a snack break in "the wet room." In this, the deepest room of the cavern, according to Bob, a small waterfall cascaded musically from a hole in one wall to splash into a small stream that ran through a trench in the rocky floor and disappeared into yet another natural opening. The stream looked innocuous enough, yet his companions informed Alex that during heavy rains, the water could turn treacherous, filling rooms, rushing through the cavern with enough force to sweep an unwary caver away.

This room, too, was filled with awesome formations, one wall almost covered with flowing draperies, the ceiling covered with stalactites and pipe straws. Alex had never fancied himself a writer, but the otherworldly appearance of these rarely seen rooms had him weaving stories in his head about unknown civilizations who might live in such surroundings. He thought of the many people above ground who'd never even dreamed such magnificence existed beneath their feet.

Debbie settled onto a flat spot on the floor, characteristically complaining about her aching muscles and damp clothes but looking as though she were enjoying herself, anyway. Bob quickly—and rather pointedly—stationed himself close to Debbie, so close, in fact, that their knees touched. Alex couldn't have sat next to Debbie if he'd wanted to, which was obviously Bob's intention.

Alex found Bob's sudden show of possessiveness as amusing as it was unwarranted.

The only other place to sit comfortably was a relatively flat spot of floor close to the waterfall, a couple of yards from where Debbie and Bob had settled. Carly folded her legs beneath her, set her gloves aside and dug into her pack. Alex lowered himself next to her, his pack beside him.

An outside observer, he reflected, would see two couples on a friendly outing. A double date in a cave. Even knowing that no such arrangement had been intended, Alex found himself enjoying the imagery, inching just a bit closer to Carly as he said, "You were right. This *is* an interesting way to spend a day."

She pulled out her water bottle and the plastic baby bottle filled with trail mix. "That's why we do it."

He'd learned the trick of looking at her without shining his headlamp directly into her eyes. He tipped his helmet back on his head and studied her. Her cheeks were slightly flushed, the hair that showed beneath her helmet damp and disheveled. Her practical layers of clothing were muddy and wrinkled, and there was a streak of mud across her right cheek.

And Alex was aware of a half-serious urge to drag her into a secluded cubbyhole and crush her soft mouth beneath his.

He cleared his throat and took a sip of his own water, washing some of the musty taste out of his mouth.

Carly nodded toward his pack. "You should eat something. Moving through a cave uses more energy than you realize. The high-protein snacks help replace some of it so that you don't overtire yourself."

"I'm not really very hungry."

"You will be before we're finished. The next couple of rooms are the most physically challenging. You'll need the extra calorie boost."

Alex shrugged and reached for his snack. "Why baby bottles?" he asked, unscrewing the top to discover the nipple upside down inside.

"The bottle is inexpensive, unbreakable, easy to pack and easy to grip. The rubber nipple provides a sanitary, waterproof seal. Why *not* use baby bottles?"

"When you put it that way, it makes sense," Alex acknowledged. "Have you had any official training in this?"

"Bob has. He belongs to the National Speleological Society, and he usually attends their national convention. Most of what I've learned has come from Bob."

Alex glanced across the room to where Bob sat talking quietly to Debbie as they ate and rested. "You and Bob seem to be good friends."

"Yes. We met when he moved into his house a few years ago. I consider him one of my closest friends."

Alex swallowed a handful of nuts and fruit. "Have he and Debbie known each other that long?"

"No. They met a little over a year ago, when Debbie came to work for me."

Keeping his voice low, Alex asked, "Did he fall for her from the beginning, or is that a new development?"

"Bob and Debbie are good friends," Carly answered primly, her tone obviously gossip squelching.

"Bob's pie-eyed over her," Alex replied bluntly. "Look at him over there. Like a rooster guarding his favorite hen from a marauding fox."

"I don't really see you as a fox. A wolf, maybe."

Alex grinned.

Carly looked at him repressively. "That wasn't meant as a compliment."

"I know."

Bob raised his voice a bit over the sound of the running water to catch Alex's attention. "Hey, Alex. Want to see what it's like down here when there aren't any human intruders? Everyone turn off your headlamps."

Simultaneously, they reached up to do so. The darkness that followed was absolute, not even a glimmer of light penetrating so far beneath the ground. Smells intensified, and the water's splashing seemed to grow louder. Alex lost all sense of direction and proportion as the room seemed to close around him. He'd gotten a bit warm while moving through the cave, but now that they were still, the damp chill began to penetrate his layers of clothing.

He wasn't claustrophobic or afraid of the dark, but he was glad to know that the light would return with only a flick of a switch.

With the lights still turned off, Bob regaled them with a tale of ancient cave explorers who braved the darkness barefoot with only primitive torches to light their way. Modern speleologists had found the evidence of those early adventurers—cave drawings, abandoned torches. Skeletons.

Debbie snapped on her light. "Enough of that talk," she said firmly. "Shouldn't we get moving again before we stiffen up?"

Turning on his own light, Bob stood and offered Debbie a hand up. "You're probably right. Let's go. Up to some belly-crawling, Alex? We'll be wading across this stream, and then the next two rooms are accessible only by passages that are basically narrow, tube-shaped openings through walls and breakdown piles."

Alex reached up to his helmet, watching as Carly's face was suddenly illuminated again. "I'm ready," he said, more confident all the time about his budding caving skills. And about his suspicion that Carly Fletcher was as interested in him as he was in her.

It wasn't long after their break that Alex got stuck.

He'd been belly-crawling in a long, narrow opening through a deep breakdown pile when his shoulders became wedged between two oddly shaped boulders. He didn't think much of it at first—after all, Bob and Debbie and Carly had gone through easily enough. For the first time since they'd entered, Alex had been bringing up the rear.

He shifted his weight, trying to move one shoulder slightly ahead of the other.

Nothing happened.

"Alex?" From somewhere ahead of him, Carly sounded only mildly concerned. "You coming?"

"Yeah, just a minute." He pushed a little harder, trying to dig into the slippery rock beneath him with his booted toes. His arms were bent beneath him. He tried pushing with his elbows to give him more of a boost forward, but his broad shoulders remained solidly jammed into the tight space.

"What's the holdup back there? Bad place to stop for a rest, Alex," Bob called from the darkness beyond.

Alex let out a breath, as if the air inside him took

up too much space, and struggled again to free himself. Absolutely nothing happened.

"Alex?" Carly sounded a bit more worried this time. "What's wrong?"

"I'm stuck," he muttered between clenched teeth, hating to have to admit it. "What should I do?"

"Where are you caught? Your shoulders?"

"Yeah."

"Maybe you should just back out. It might be too tight for you."

No kidding. "I'll try."

But Alex was as incapable of moving backward as he was forward. He was stuck tighter than a cork in a bottle. He tried to be wryly amused. He was certain this slightly embarrassing incident would be short-lived. All he had to do was twist a certain way and he'd be free.

But no matter which way he twisted, he didn't move. And he was beginning to get angry—as well as a bit panicky, a fact he was determined to hide.

Carly had crawled back to him now, her headlamp shining into his eyes. He squinted at it. She reached up to tip it back, making Alex aware that the passage was considerably wider just beyond where he'd gotten stuck.

If he had only made it a few more inches…

"You really are stuck, aren't you?" Carly asked, studying him closely.

He sighed as deeply as his confined space allowed. "That's what I said."

"You can't move backward?"

"I can't move at *all.*"

"Try moving one shoulder at a time."

"Tried it," he muttered, but tried again, to no avail.

"Put your head down and shove yourself backward as hard as you can."

He did. "Nothing."

Her face close to his, Carly frowned. "Maybe I should back out and let Bob come in."

"No!" He shook his head, the only movement he was capable of making at the moment. "Don't bring Bob into this." He would never hear the end of it if Bob saw him wedged in the rock like a pimento in an olive, he thought grimly.

More determined than ever to get himself unstuck, he redoubled his efforts, squirming and pushing until he was panting with exertion. "Damn it!"

"Everything okay in there?" Bob called, his voice echoing strangely in the depths of the cavern.

"Fine," Carly called back. "Alex's shoulders are too wide for this passage. He and I are going back. You and Debbie take your time."

"Okay. Wait for us by the waterfall. We've found a new opening we want to check out, and we'll be there shortly."

"Take your time," Carly repeated.

"Thanks," Alex said gratefully.

"It's Debbie's teasing I'm saving you from, not Bob's," she answered wryly. "We may still have to call for help, though, if we can't get you out of here."

"I'll get out of here if I have to remove an arm or chew through the rock." Though Alex was teasing, his tone was grimmer than he'd intended. He could almost feel the cave growing smaller around him, taking his air, seeming to squeeze him until he could hardly breathe.

Carly's eyes narrowed as she studied his face. "I

thought you said you didn't have a problem with claustrophobia."

"I don't. I just don't like being unable to move."

His arms were going dead beneath him. He had an unpleasant sensation that slimy, blind cave bugs were crawling up his pant legs. He wanted out. He wanted out *now*.

"Alex?" Carly's voice seemed to come from farther away, though she hadn't moved. "Alex, look at me."

He lifted his head, looked into the face illuminated by the reflected light of their combined headlamps, which now pointed upward. Her pupils were dilated to make the most of the dim light, making her eyes look darker and bigger in her pale face. A strand of silky, dark blond hair escaped from beneath her helmet to caress her temple. The smudge of mud was still on her cheek. If Alex could move, he would have reached out to stroke it gently away.

"Okay, take a deep breath," she said.

"If I could do that, I could get out of here."

She smiled faintly, apparently satisfied by his reasonable tone. "I thought you were about to panic. I was trying to calm you down."

One corner of his mouth lifted in an attempt to return the smile. "Nah. Though if I'd thought of it, I might have faked a panic attack to see if you would kiss me to calm me down."

"Now I *am* worried about you. You're getting delirious."

Still lying on her stomach, she reached between them and placed her hands on his shoulders. "Okay, I'm going to prop my feet on this outcropping of rock behind me and push. You shove backward with your hands as hard as you can.''

''Wait.''

''What? Is something hurting you?''

''Scoot a little closer to me. That will give you more leverage.''

Though she looked a bit suspicious, she seemed to accept his reasoning. She inched a bit closer, her hands still on his shoulders, her face only an inch from his.

Stretching his neck, Alex pressed a quick kiss against her lips. ''Okay,'' he said. ''Now I'm ready to try again.''

Carly looked flustered, less in command of the situation. Rather pleased with himself, Alex pulled his shoulders in as far as possible without risking dislocation, planted his gloved hands flatly beneath him and shoved backward as hard as he could. Carly pushed.

A few uncomfortable moments later, he was free, panting with the exertion but greatly relieved. He worked his way backward through the passage until his feet were dangling into the tiny room behind him. Another push and he dropped out of the passage and was on his feet, his head only a couple of inches beneath the low ceiling of the cramped room. He nearly bopped his helmet against a low-hanging stalactite, but his ordeal hadn't taken away his regard for the cave's delicate features.

Carly came out of the passage, landing gracefully on her heavy boots. ''Are you okay?''

He shrugged. ''I'm fine. Probably would have gotten out on my own in another few minutes.''

''No doubt,'' she agreed dryly.

"So," he said, stepping closer to her so that she was forced to back against the rock wall behind her, "what shall we do to entertain ourselves until the others rejoin us?"

"We'll rest," she said.

"Exactly what I had in mind," he assured her, and lowered his head. Their helmets bumped together when he covered her mouth with his. The beams from their headlights merged to form one light. Alex rather fancied the imagery.

Carly didn't immediately pull back. He wasn't sure if that was because she liked his kiss or because he'd backed her against the wall and she had nowhere else to go, but he didn't want to question his luck. He kissed her again.

This was ridiculous, Carly thought. They were standing in a hole in the ground, wearing muddy clothes, thick gloves and heavy plastic helmets. The air was damp and musty, smelling of mud and bat droppings. The light from their headlamps was stark and yellow within the absolute darkness. There shouldn't be anything in the least romantic about those circumstances. And yet, she found herself being seduced with nothing more than Alex's kisses.

His mouth was warm in comparison with the chilly air. He stood as close to her as possible without actually pressing her against the rock behind her...and still she was tempted to pull him closer. He was tall and solid and radiated warmth and strength. The broad shoulders that had become wedged in the rocks now seemed to invite her to rest her head on them.

Her gloved hands were actually lifting to go around his neck when she made herself stop and be sensible. She drew her head back from his, reluctantly breaking the kiss. "We shouldn't be doing this," she murmured, her voice husky.

"Why not?"

To her chagrin, she didn't have an immediate answer to that simple question. The best she could come up with was, "Bob and Debbie will be back in a minute."

Alex's mouth quirked into that faint half smile that Carly secretly found so devastating. "Bob and Debbie are probably doing the same thing wherever they are."

Carly knew better than that, but she had no intention of discussing her friends' complex relationship with Alex. Instead, she placed a hand on his chest and gave a slight backward push, needing some distance between them so that she could clear her mind.

Obligingly, he stepped back. She noted the clearly hand-shaped imprint her filthy glove had left on his chest. It gave her the strangest feeling that he carried part of her away with him.

She chided herself for being silly. She wasn't usually so foolishly fanciful. Alex Keating, this man who was, after all, little more than a stranger to her, had certainly *not* stolen her heart in the few short days she'd known him.

It was ridiculous to even imagine that he had, she told herself firmly. The musty air in this cavern must be going to her helmeted head.

Bob and Debbie rejoined them a short while later. Alex recognized the look on Bob's face as that of a man who'd taken a chance and gotten shot down. Debbie wore no expression whatever, so Alex still had no clue how she really felt about the man she held so firmly at arm's length.

Alex wasn't entirely dissatisfied with the progress he'd made while he and Carly had been alone. She had definitely responded to his kisses—before she'd pushed him away. Her signals were still mixed, but he no longer doubted that she was affected by him, even though her wariness was obvious.

He couldn't blame her for her caution, of course. She hardly knew him. She had no idea what his intentions were toward her. Which made sense, since Alex had no clue himself what it was he wanted from Carly Fletcher.

He just knew he wanted her. But she didn't seem the type for a vacation fling, and he wasn't sure that was what he wanted from her, anyway. He was as confused by what had developed between them as Carly seemed to be.

Still, he had no intention of avoiding her for the duration of his time here. Maybe it was best to just play it by ear, follow his instincts—which were, even now, urging him to move closer to her.

Wearing a smile that looked rather strained, Bob turned to Alex. "Sorry, Alex. I thought you'd be able to make it through that passage."

"I gave it a good try," Alex replied lightly, glad that Bob and Debbie had missed seeing him so ignominiously stuck.

Debbie patted his left arm. "First time those broad shoulders of yours proved a handicap, I'd bet."

There was a slight edge to her teasing this time. A message Alex knew was not directed at him. Refusing to be pulled into whatever game she was playing with

Bob, he only shrugged and moved slightly away from her. "Where do we go now?"

"Back out the way we came," Bob said. "We've gone as far as we can today."

Alex wondered if Bob's words could be taken two ways. And he couldn't help hoping that he wasn't looking at Carly with the same revealingly wistful expression Bob wore every time he glanced Debbie's way.

Six

Less than fifteen minutes after Bob drove into his driveway, Carly and Debbie were gone, leaving Alex and Bob alone. Watching Carly disappear into her house after she'd made a hasty excuse about needing to telephone the hospital to check on a patient, Alex sighed and turned to Bob, who'd been watching the dust from Debbie's car settle on the road.

Weren't they a fine pair?

Alex pushed his hands into his pockets. "Thanks for asking me to join you today. It was an... interesting experience."

Bob nodded a bit glumly. "Carly and Debbie seemed to enjoy having you along."

Alex thought it was time to make something perfectly clear. "I'm sure you know that Debbie likes to tease. She's no more interested in me on a personal level than I am in her."

After only a momentary hesitation, Bob sighed faintly and nodded. "I know. Not that it would be any of my business if you *were* interested in each other, of course."

"Struck out with her, huh?" Alex's tone was pure guy-to-guy commiseration.

"Repeatedly," Bob agreed, his own words wry. "She's made it very clear that she likes me well enough, but she can't deal with my job."

That took Alex by surprise. No matter what else he might think of Debbie McElroy, he never would have expected her to be a snob. "What's wrong with being a carpenter?"

Now it was Bob's turn to look surprised. "A carpenter?"

Alex gestured toward the workshop in which he and Bob had first met. "Well, aren't you?"

Bob's smile was crooked. "Yes. But that's my supplementary job—the one that pays my bills. It's my other career that Debbie objects to."

"And what is that?"

"I'm pastor of the Friendship Church of Seventy-Six. It's a little nondenominational church with about a hundred members."

"Oh." Alex couldn't think of anything else to say.

Bob was a minister. Alex hadn't even considered that possibility before, and he found himself quickly reviewing everything he'd said in the other man's presence. Had he said anything offensive?

Bob rubbed his dirt-smudged chin. "Sorry. I guess I assumed Carly or Betty had mentioned it. They're both members of my congregation."

Alex shook his head. "It never came up, I suppose. Still, I don't see the problem. Is Debbie of a different religion?"

"It isn't that. She just has no interest in being involved with a pastor. Too much pressure, she says. And no matter what my feelings for her, I can't change what I am."

Alex nodded, thinking of the women who'd been unable to cope with the demands of his own career. The broken dates and missed parties, the canceled vacations and his deep distraction when a particularly difficult case occupied his mind for days at a time.

Not once had Alex ever considered changing in any way to please those women, and he'd never fancied himself in love with any of them. He could imagine how difficult it must be for Bob to be in love with a woman who couldn't accept his calling.

"You need any help putting the rest of this stuff away?"

Bob shook his head. "Thanks, but I can take it from here. You'll probably want to go take a hot bath. Trust me, you used muscles today that are going to protest later."

"I believe you." Surreptitiously, Alex flexed his right shoulder, which he suspected bore a bruise from his close encounter with the narrow rock passage. He was going to be carrying some colorful physical souvenirs home from this vacation, he thought, touching his discolored temple as he walked toward his rental car. If he wasn't careful about Carly, his ego might take a few blows, as well.

He refused to even consider the possibility that his heart was at risk. That was one part of himself that Alex had always taken great care to protect.

"Did you have a good time today, dear?" Betty asked after Carly had showered, dressed in clean clothing and put away her caving gear.

"Yes, very nice." Carly opened the refrigerator and poured a glass of orange juice, which she carried to the table, where her grandmother sat with a cup of coffee. "Exhausting, as always, but fun. Bob found a new passage he wants to explore, but it was beyond a point Alex couldn't get through, so he decided to wait until next time.''

''Alex had trouble?'' Betty frowned in quick concern. ''That surprises me. He looks to be in such good shape.''

Carly chuckled weakly, picturing Alex's great shape in vivid detail. ''That wasn't the problem,'' she replied a bit dryly. ''His shoulders are too wide. He got thoroughly wedged into a narrow passage. I had to help push him out of it. We didn't tell Debbie about it, for obvious reasons.''

''She would tease him mercilessly, wouldn't she? I won't tell her, either. How did Alex handle it?''

Carly thought of the quick flare of panic she'd seen in Alex's eyes, and the way he'd almost immediately masked it behind masculine bravado. Alex Keating wasn't one to display his emotions, she mused. And she'd already known that he disliked showing his weaknesses. Had the parents who'd disliked family vacations been the type to demand perfection from their only son?

She shook her head, slightly embarrassed by her amateur attempts to analyze Alex. She really was going to have to stop spending so much time thinking about him. She'd thought of little else since Burle and Jeff had hauled him into her clinic.

Remembering that her grandmother had asked a question, Carly said, ''Alex handled everything fine. He seemed to enjoy it. More than he expected, I think.''

''I'm glad. I think he needs to have more fun, don't you? I have a feeling he's one of those workaholic types who doesn't take nearly enough time for himself. When I asked if he'd ever been married, he said no, that he'd always been too busy with his career. He said this is the first vacation he's taken in years.''

Carly wasn't surprised that Betty had asked such a personal question of their guest; her grandmother's curiosity was as avid as it was harmless. Carly doubted that Alex had been offended, since he'd seemed fond of Betty. ''Did he mention what he does back in Boston?'' she asked, her own curiosity overcoming her distaste for gossip.

''Careerwise?'' Betty thought about it a moment, then shook her head. ''No, not specifically. I just assumed he's into big business.''

Carly nodded. ''I've guessed the same thing. He doesn't talk much about himself.''

''He said his parents will be spending the winter in Italy. I get the impression that Alex spends a lot of time alone. Do you think he's a bit shy?''

Thinking of several expertly stolen kisses, Carly laughed dryly. ''No, Granny, I don't think Alex is at all shy. I have a feeling that any time he spends alone is strictly by choice.''

Betty tapped her cheek with one finger. ''He is a very attractive man, isn't he?''

''He's quite handsome,'' Carly agreed, trying to sound casual.

''Have you noticed how dark his eyes are? Such a deep blue they're almost navy. And those shoulders… Let's just say I wasn't a bit surprised that he had trouble fitting them into a narrow space.''

''Granny,'' Carly said warningly, sensing what was coming.

''He has a good heart, Carly. I can tell about things like that, you know.''

Carly didn't have to be reminded that her grandmother had never liked Linc. She'd said all along that Linc had dishonest eyes. And she'd been right. But if Betty was trying to do some matchmaking now, she was being totally unrealistic.

"He seems to like you," Betty added, leaving no further doubt of her intentions.

Carly shook her head. "Not interested, Granny."

Betty snorted inelegantly. "I don't believe you."

"He lives in Boston, remember? That's a long way from here—both literally and figuratively. I know you're getting pretty desperate lately to fix me up with someone—anyone—but this match is too far-fetched even for you."

Betty sighed deeply. "I am not desperate to fix you up. I've simply pointed out a few times that you aren't getting any younger. If you're going to have those children you've always wanted, you're going to have to find yourself a husband."

"Who says a woman has to have a husband to have children?" Carly asked, a bit tauntingly. "Not a very modern attitude, Granny."

Her grandmother narrowed her eyes and shook a slightly bent finger in Carly's direction. "I'm not a very modern woman. And neither are you, Carlene Elizabeth Fletcher, so don't let me hear you talking that way, you hear?"

"Yes, ma'am," Carly agreed with feigned meekness. "But you still have to admit that Alex Keating and I are an unlikely couple."

Betty nodded reluctantly. "I suppose you're right. Still, it can't hurt for you to be nice to him while he's here. I'm sure you'd both have a very nice time together."

"Whatever you say, Granny." Carly drained her

orange juice and rose to set her glass in the dishwasher. She paused in the doorway to give her grandmother an impish look. "Um...just how 'nice' would you like me to be to Mr. Keating?"

Again, that grandmotherly finger shook in Carly's direction. "Don't make me go out and cut a hickory switch, Carlene."

Carly was laughing when she left the room. She heard her grandmother chuckling ruefully behind her.

Despite the activities of the day, Alex didn't sleep very well Saturday night. Every time he crawled beneath the covers, he ended up tossing and turning on the somewhat lumpy bed. He tried to blame his sore muscles, his still-tender head, all the other various bumps and bruises he'd somehow acquired on his vacation. But the truth was, he couldn't stop thinking about Carly Fletcher.

Odd. No woman had ever taken over his thoughts this way. As he sat in a chair, an unopened book in his lap, the corners of the room thrown into deep shadows by the single lamp burning beside him, he told himself that he couldn't stop thinking about her only because there was nothing else to occupy his mind at the moment. At home, he lost himself in his work, leaving him little time to think about anything else, his women friends included. Here, he had nothing to do but listen to the crickets chirp and remember the sweet taste of Carly's mouth.

Sometime around dawn, he came to the conclusion that it would be best to avoid her for the duration of his vacation. He'd come to fish. To relax. Catch up on his reading, both for business and pleasure. Maybe do some hiking.

And he'd come to be alone, he reminded himself. That had seemed like a desirable state to be in last week, when he'd been inundated with meetings, patients, telephone messages, E-mail, faxes, social obligations, the constant beeping of his pager and bleating of his cell phone.

So why did it seem so damn lonely now? He glared at the silent, empty room around him and forced himself to open the book.

You're getting old, Keating. That fortieth birthday has gone right to the old gray matter.

It was hunger that drove him out of the cabin at just before noon the next day. None of the quick snack meals he'd stocked appealed to him. He wanted hot food, preferably something he didn't have to cook himself.

There weren't many restaurants to choose from in tiny Seventy-Six, Arkansas. He settled for a steak house on the main highway. The number of cars already gathering in the parking lot hinted that the food wasn't bad. Running a hand through his hair, he hoped his denim shirt and jeans were appropriate attire. He had at least taken the time to shave before heading out into public.

He needn't have worried about his clothing, he decided the minute he stepped into the rustic lobby. This was hardly a formal-attire establishment. The diners seated inside were casually dressed; Alex thought it must be a bit too early for the after-church crowd, if this was one of their favored destinations.

''Hey,'' a heavyset woman in tight red stretch pants greeted him. ''How many?''

''Just one.''

''Smokin'?''

"Nonsmoking," he corrected.

She snatched up a plastic-coated menu from a tray on the checkout desk and moved away from him with swaying hips. "This way," she called over her shoulder.

The decor inside the dining room was Early Dead Animal, Alex decided with a stifled smile. Mounted, glassy-eyed heads of assorted species loomed over the tables, interspersed with dusty fish attached to wooden plaques. The wooden tables were covered with red-and-white-checked plastic, and the piped-in music was twangy country.

Alex had a feeling the menu would be as unpretentious as the furnishings. Meat and potatoes, most likely. A couple of vegetables to choose from, if he was lucky.

He'd hardly taken his seat at a table set for four when he heard a familiar voice say, "Well, hey there, slick."

Alex looked up to find Debbie McElroy standing beside him, hands on her slender hips, her copper head tilted as she looked at him with raised eyebrows.

"Hi, Debbie. Fancy seeing you again so soon."

She grimaced. "It's not like there are that many places to go around here. It's more surprising when you *don't* run into people you know every time you step outside."

Studying her expression, Alex smiled. "And I thought you said you don't have a problem with claustrophobia."

She gave one of her rare laughs. "Not in caves," she admitted. "Only in very small towns."

"Are you meeting someone for lunch?"

"No. This place belongs to my aunt and uncle. I

come here frequently because they feed me for free. And because I can't boil water for myself."

Alex motioned toward the empty chairs at his table. "Would you like to join me? Or would you rather dine alone today for the sake of that small-town claustrophobia?"

She slid into the empty chair directly across from him. "Doesn't apply to you," she explained. "I haven't known you long enough to be bored by your stories yet."

"I don't tell stories."

"Well, there you go. Even better."

Alex glanced at his menu. "What do you recommend for lunch?"

"Leaving town. But since you're already here, have a steak. There's not much they can do to mess up a grilled steak."

"Tell me, Deb, have you always had this sunny, optimistic disposition, or is it something you've had to work at?"

Again, Debbie gave a sharp bark of laughter. "Shut up and order, Keating," she said, motioning for a harried-looking young server.

After they'd made their choices and had been left alone again, Debbie said, "We're certainly giving them something to talk about now."

Alex glanced automatically at the other diners, many of whom seemed to be surreptitiously looking back at him. "What are we doing?"

"We're sitting together. At the same table." Debbie spoke with an exaggerated breathlessness, making the innocent words sound strangely salacious.

Alex chuckled. "I don't think your town is so old-fashioned as to find it shocking when a man and a woman dine at the same table.''

''Oh, it isn't that. They just love to gossip. Speculate. Weave stories about who's doing what to whom, and how often. Anything to alleviate the boredom. Coming from a big city like Boston, you can't imagine what it's like to have everything you do watched and talked about, to know that you can't go anywhere that you don't run into half a dozen people you know, that anything you say or do will be talked about all over town the next day.''

Wincing, Alex thought of the embarrassing celebrity he'd encountered after that ridiculous article had been published in *Prominence Magazine,* naming him one of the world's most eligible bachelors. He'd deliberately chosen to vacation in a secluded, rural area where the residents would be more likely to read *Field and Stream* than *Prominence Magazine,* hoping for a couple of weeks of blissful anonymity.

''Boston's smaller than you might realize in some ways,'' he murmured, thinking of how often he was recognized.

''No way is Boston like Seventy-Six, Arkansas,'' Debbie argued with a firm shake of her head.

Deciding not to argue with her, Alex propped his elbows on the table and leaned forward slightly. ''Do you really dislike living here so much?''

She started to answer immediately, then paused, shook her head and sighed. ''I'm in a particularly lousy mood today, I guess. Obviously, if I hated it here that badly, I'd leave. I'm just having…personal problems at the moment.''

Alex was pretty sure he knew what—or whom—those personal problems involved. Debbie's expression looked very much like the one Bob had worn after the caving outing yesterday.

Alex made a point never to get involved in other people's private lives. Friends, acquaintances, family, patients.... He neither asked for nor offered advice, didn't ask personal questions, rarely shared his own problems. Self-sufficiency had been the word in his family. One handled one's own business and left others to handle theirs.

Yet something in Debbie's unhappy eyes propelled him to ask a bit awkwardly, "Would you like to talk about it?"

"No, thanks. I'm not one to carry on about my personal problems," Debbie answered, energetically stirring sugar into her iced tea. And then, "Did Bob talk about me after I left yesterday?"

"In what respect?" Alex asked guardedly.

Debbie gave him a chiding look. "In any respect."

Feeling caught in the middle, Alex phrased his answer with care. "He seems to hold you in high regard."

Debbie grinned fleetingly. "That highbrowed accent of yours is sure sexy, slick. No wonder Carly just about swallows her tongue every time you speak. Anyway, what I want to know is, did Bob tell you that he fancies himself in love with me?"

"Er..." Caught off guard by Debbie's offhand comment about Carly—did she really find his accent appealing?—Alex answered without stopping to think. "Yes, he...I mean, I suspected...uh..."

"Never mind." Debbie shook her head and sighed again. "It's not like he makes any big secret of it. Compulsive honesty is part of Bob's business."

"He, um, mentioned that his 'business' is part of

the problem. He said it bothers you that he's a minister."

"Bob's a natural-born preacher man," Debbie admitted, sounding resigned to that fact. "He's just good, you know? All the way through. Too good for the likes of me, if only he'd accept it."

"Bob doesn't strike me as a fool, Debbie. I'm sure he's a better judge of character than you're giving him credit for."

The server reappeared, bearing two metal plates holding incredibly large steaks and oversize baked potatoes dripping with enough butter and sour cream to give a self-respecting cardiologist a twinge of guilt before he dived in.

"Who's your friend, Deb?" the young woman asked, sliding the plates in front of them.

"Alex Keating, meet my cousin, Mildred McElroy," Debbie said curtly.

Alex murmured a polite greeting, which Mildred returned with open curiosity as she looked from Alex to her cousin and back again. "Mom said to tell y'all to enjoy your meal and she'll be over to say hello as soon as she gets a minute."

Debbie nodded. "I'm sure she will. Be prepared," she added to Alex when her cousin had hurried away. "Aunt Edna will probably ask all kinds of questions that are none of her business. She's the biggest gossip in town. Good-hearted, but she's got a mouth that never stops flappin'. Just start talking about the weather or something if she gets too nosy."

Alex sliced into his steak. "I have some experience in dealing with gossip. I can handle it."

"I bet you do," Debbie murmured, studying him

appraisingly. "You don't talk about yourself much, do you, Alex?"

Chewing his steak, he shrugged, letting that gesture serve as his answer.

Debbie nodded and sprinkled salt on her potato. "Me, either. I'm not one of those blabbermouths who'll tell her whole life story to a stranger on a plane. Not that I've been on many planes, but the last time I was on one...I think I was on my way to my uncle Joe's funeral in Atlanta...anyway, there was this woman beside me that thought I wanted to know every little detail of her life. Didn't matter how rude I was, she just kept talking. Before we landed, I knew everything but how much she weighed, and I could've guessed that within five pounds or so."

"Yes, I've been..."

"Thought her life was so interesting. Yeah, right. Compared to my life, hers was right out of a TV sitcom. I got married when I was seventeen to a rodeo cowboy. Bet you didn't know that, did you, slick?"

Alex swallowed a bite of steak. "No, I..."

"His name was Bo. He could charm the red off a peppermint stick. My daddy hated him. Bo talked me into running off with him halfway through my senior year of high school. We spent the next five years wandering around the country, following the rodeo circuit, drinking and partying and fighting. I finally left him when he got skunk drunk one night and beat the crap out of me. I moved to Little Rock, went to nursing school during the day and served drinks in bars at night to pay my way. I worked in Pine Bluff for a while, until Aunt Edna told me that Carly's nurse had got married and moved out of state and that Carly was looking for someone to replace her. I liked the idea of working with a woman doctor instead of the sexist creep I worked for in Pine Bluff, so I decided to give it a shot.''

Amused, Alex continued to eat without trying to interrupt again. It was a good thing, he thought ruefully, that Debbie wasn't one to talk about her personal life. Who knew *what* she would tell him if she was?

''Now, tell me,'' Debbie demanded. ''Does that sound like the background of a preacher's wife?''

''Well...''

''I told Bob all about it, of course, when he started asking me out. I figured he should know the whole story, even though I don't like talking about my past. I thought he'd back off quick enough once he knew where I'd come from, but he didn't. He kept saying it didn't matter, that all he cared about was who I am now. Can you believe it?''

Eating in quick, choppy movements between words, Debbie scowled, seeming to take little pleasure in her food. ''I'm aware that other folks in town have tried to talk him out of pursuing me. I'm sure they've told him he can do better. I know they've tried to fix him up with all the available women in the area—not that there are that many to choose from around here. But he just won't listen.''

''He's a man who knows what he wants,'' Alex murmured, taking advantage of an opportunity to speak when Debbie took a bite of her steak. ''You have to admire that.''

''I admire a lot of things about Bob,'' Debbie muttered. ''I just—''

''Hey, Deb.'' A grizzled-looking man in a cap and plaid shirt bulging over the waistband of inexpensive jeans nodded as he sauntered up to the table. "How's it going?"

"Fine, Gus. And you?"

"Can't complain. Much," he added with a tobacco-stained grin.

"You coming in to get that blood pressure checked this week?"

"I reckon you'll come after me if I don't."

"You got that straight."

Gus chuckled and glanced at Alex. "She's little, but she's mean."

"Get yourself out of here, Gus. We're trying to eat."

Unoffended, the man waved and ambled away.

"Now," Debbie said, turning back to Alex. "About you and Carly—"

Immediately wary, Alex asked suspiciously, "What about us?"

"I saw you looking at her like she was the last piece of pie and you were just coming off a seven-day fast. And she must have blushed about a dozen times yesterday, which is hardly like her. You're not one of those guys who thinks he's got to bag a pretty woman in every town he visits, are you?"

Alex frowned. "Damn it, Debbie. What kind of question is that?"

She shrugged. "Seemed simple enough to me. Are you?"

"No, I'm not trying to 'bag' Carly. I like her. I find her attractive. But that's the extent of it."

And he didn't even know why he'd admitted that much to this woman. Something about Debbie McElroy made him say things he had no intention of saying. It would serve her right if he started giving her advice about Bob. Something along the lines of telling her to quit being a fool and grab a good man while she had the chance. He had opened his mouth to do just that when the heavyset woman in red stretch pants approached the table, carrying two massive pieces of coconut cream pie topped high with golden meringue.

"Brought y'all some dessert," she said. "Introduce me to your friend, Deborah."

Alex decided later, on his way back to his cabin, that it was just as well Debbie's aunt had chosen that moment to make her appearance. There'd been little chance for private conversation after that. After finishing dessert, Alex had insisted on paying for his meal and Debbie's, avoiding personal questions by blandly chatting about how nice the weather had been during his visit. And then he'd escaped.

He found himself liking Debbie McElroy more than he'd expected from his first impression of her. He could see why Bob was taken with her. Not that Alex had any personal interest in her. Carly was the one who still occupied his thoughts, no matter how he tried to distract himself.

This vacation was turning out to be a great deal different than he could ever have anticipated when he'd made his plans in Boston.

Seven

Carly's waiting room was filled with patients Monday morning. And it seemed as though every one of them mentioned that her nurse had been spotted having a cozy Sunday lunch with a handsome, dark-haired stranger.

"You should have seen him, Dr. Fletcher," a heavily pregnant young woman whispered avidly as Carly palpated her baby-filled stomach. "Dark hair and dark blue eyes. A dimple in his chin. You don't see guys like that around here very often. He was so good-looking I could hardly concentrate on my lunch. Andy was about to get jealous."

Carly felt her pulse jerk. It didn't take three guesses for her to figure out who Debbie's dining companion had been. She couldn't help wondering when and how that arrangement had come about. Had the two met by accident at the restaurant owned by Debbie's relatives? Or—and Carly couldn't help remembering the flirting Debbie and Alex had carried on Saturday—had an invitation been extended and accepted?

Was Alex the type who would kiss one woman and ask another to lunch?

Nancy's baby kicked Carly's hand, drawing her thoughts back to her job. "Everything looks fine, Nancy. It won't be much longer before you'll be holding this little one in your arms."

"I'm ready for that," Nancy said fervently. "I'm beginning to wonder if I'll ever see my feet again."

"It'll be over before you know it." Carly lowered Debbie's loose-fitting maternity top and helped her sit upright on the examination table.

"That's what Andy said. He took me out to eat yesterday 'cause he said who knew when we'd be able to go out just the two of us like that again. We're both real excited about the baby, but we know it'll mean a lot of changes."

Carly suspected her smile was bittersweet. How many babies had she delivered in the past few years? How many times had she wondered if she would ever know that joy for herself? Wondered if she would ever find the time or the opportunity to have a family of her own.

Sending Nancy on her way, Carly moved into the next examining room, where Debbie was taking Gus Eberle's blood pressure. "How's it going, Gus?" Carly asked, noting Debbie's frown.

"Pretty good, Doc. How're things with you?"

"Can't complain." Carly glanced over Debbie's shoulder as the nurse wrote Gus's blood pressure reading onto his chart. "Have you been taking your medications, Gus?"

"Oh, yeah, sure," her patient answered breezily. And then, when Carly turned to look at him, he cleared his throat. "Well, most of the time. When I remember. And I've cut back on the cigarettes, Doc. Down to a pack a day."

Carly nodded. "I'm glad you're trying, but your blood pressure is still high enough for concern. I'd like you to try to cut down even more on the cigarettes—quit completely, if you can. And figure out some system that will help you remember to take your medications. This is very important, Gus. You and I have talked about the risk of a stroke or heart attack if you aren't more careful.''

''I'll try,'' Gus muttered, hanging his head. ''It's just hard to give up habits I've had for nearly fifty years now.''

Carly patted his arm affectionately. ''I know. I want to see you again in a couple of days, okay? We need to keep a close eye on this blood pressure of yours.''

He nodded glumly, then looked at Debbie, who'd been putting away the blood pressure cuff, making more notes on Gus's chart and listening to every word. ''You better keep an eye on your nurse here, Doc. Next thing you know, she'll be running off and getting married like that last one did. I seen her eating dinner with a fine-looking young man yesterday. They looked mighty cozy together, too.''

Carly hung on to her smile with an effort as Debbie began to scold, ''Honestly, Gus, you're worse than a gossipy old lady. I was just having lunch with a friend, and don't you be going around blabbing about it all over town, you hear? It's a pretty sad state of affairs when a body can't even have a friendly lunch without the whole town talking about it.''

Gus's faded eyes widened innocently. ''Hey, I was just making conversation. No need to get all prickly about it.''

''I'll let you two finish this in private,'' Carly interrupted hastily. ''I have other things to do. Gus, you take care of yourself and I'll see you later this week.''

''Sure thing, Doc.''

Debbie and Gus were still bantering when Carly

left the room, her smile fading as soon as she was out of their sight. She had to remind herself again that it was none of her business if Alex and Debbie had lunched together. Carly's grandmother had wanted Carly to invite Alex to share Sunday lunch with them, but Carly had refused to ask him, telling Betty that she was sure he wasn't interested in spending his entire vacation with them.

He'd obviously had no qualms about spending more time with Debbie.

"Dr. Fletcher?" Cathy Hurleman, the receptionist and cashier, hurried down the hallway, her arms loaded with a stack of color-coded manila folders. "There's a man in the lobby who says he's here to pay his bill. He says his name is Alex Keating, but I can't find a file for him."

Carly froze in her tracks. Alex was here? To pay his bill…or to see her?

Or was it possible, she wondered with a slight, sinking feeling, that Alex was here to see Debbie?

"Who else is waiting for me, Cathy?"

"You have an hour scheduled now for lunch. Mr. Keating is the only one in the waiting room."

"Bring him back to my office, please. I'd like to talk to him about his account."

Cathy nodded. "I'll be right back. By the way," she added over her shoulder, "he sure is pretty."

Carly was reminded of that quip when Alex stepped into her office a few moments later. Oh, yes, she thought wistfully. He most definitely was pretty, in an unquestionably masculine way.

His dark hair was brushed back from his forehead, revealing what remained of the four-day-old bruise at his temple. He wore a cream-colored denim shirt tucked into slim-fitting jeans and a pair of expensive-looking tooled leather boots. And he was smiling that faint, one-sided smile that always made Carly's heart trip over itself.

Surreptitiously, she straightened the white lab coat she wore over a pale blue sweater and tailored navy slacks. She resisted reaching up to check her hair.

"Hello, Carly." His voice was the one that had whispered to her in dreams she blushed now to remember.

She had to silently clear her throat before she could reply. "Hello, Alex."

He closed her office door behind him, taking a quick look around at the overfilled bookshelves, the files piled on every surface, the papers covering her desk. Her office was too small, and she'd had little time to catch up on her paperwork lately. She knew it must look terribly messy to him.

She slid her hands into her pockets, not knowing what else to do with them. "Cathy told me you asked about your bill."

"Yes." He took a step closer to her, his gaze locked with hers. "Apparently, you haven't had an opportunity to prepare one for me."

"I have no intention of billing you. I didn't do anything but apply a bandage to your forehead."

"I'm paying for your services," Alex told her adamantly. "You stayed after hours to treat me. You took me home with you, cared for me during the night and fed me the next morning. I owe you, and I intend to pay my debt."

Carly lifted her chin. "My grandmother and I don't run a bed-and-breakfast inn. You were our guest because you had no one else to watch out for you that night. We don't charge our guests."

"But you do charge your patients. At least bill me for an office call."

She hesitated. Something inside her rebelled at the thought of taking Alex's money, even for her professional services...which was really silly when she stopped to think about it.

"I'll bill you for an office call," she agreed. "Cathy will take care of it for you. It should only take a few minutes."

"Fine. Now that we have that out of the way, there's something else I need to discuss with you."

He took another step closer as he spoke, backing Carly against the desk. A detached part of her mind noted that he always seemed to be backing her against something, even as she asked, "What is it?"

"This," he said, just before covering her mouth with his.

This was something else he seemed to be doing quite a bit lately, Carly mused dazedly. And as her arms slipped around his neck, she found that she had no desire to complain.

The kiss was slow. Deep. Hungry.

Devastating.

By the time Alex lifted his head, Carly had no defenses left against him.

Her hands still resting on his shoulders, she looked up at him, aroused, confused, exasperated with his presumption and her own complicity. "Why do you keep doing that?"

His hands rested lightly at her waist. His eyes remained locked with hers, glittering, but hard to read. "I can't seem to help myself," he said, his voice a low, seductive murmur. "Every time I'm with you, all I can think of is being closer to you. You fascinate me, Carly Fletcher. I can't explain it better than that."

"I'm very attracted to you, Alex. I think you realize that."

She held him still when he would have pulled her closer. "However," she continued firmly, "I'm a very busy woman. I'm afraid I don't have time to entertain you during your vacation, if that's what you're hoping for."

She saw the temper flare in his eyes. His faint smile vanished, to be replaced by a scowl.

"I'm perfectly capable of entertaining myself during my vacation," he said curtly. "If all I wanted was companionship, I wouldn't have come here alone. I did have other options."

"I'm sure you did." Carly had no doubt that there were several women who would have loved to accompany Alex Keating on his vacation. He struck her as a man who was accustomed to women's attentions. It wasn't conceit she sensed in him exactly. More a confidence that came from experience.

Carly's own experience had left her very wary of charming men with attractive faces and enticing smiles.

"I didn't come here looking for a fling. I never expected to meet anyone who interests me the way you do. But now that we have met, is there any reason we shouldn't get to know each other better? We just might have more in common than you think."

That she doubted. A country doctor and a Boston businessman? A woman from a poor, rural background and a man whose parents spent their winters in Italy? What could they possibly have in common?

She was still standing almost in his arms. His hands were warm at her waist, his shoulders solid and strong beneath her palms. His clever mouth was so close that all she would have to do was lift herself a few inches to kiss him, and the temptation to do so was almost overwhelming.

Okay, so maybe they could find a few things in common.

"I don't have a lot of free time," she repeated, not sure if she was still trying to warn him off or simply letting him know the limitations they faced.

"I can entertain myself when you're busy," he said again. "Are you free tonight?"

She wrinkled her nose. "I have to attend a charity thing. It's a dance at the community center to raise money for upgrading equipment at the volunteer fire department. I bought a couple of tickets several weeks ago. I, er, have an extra ticket if you'd like to go with me," she added a bit hesitantly. "But I warn you, it might not be something you would enjoy."

He shrugged. "I attend a lot of charity affairs back home," he said. "It's part of my job. I'd be delighted to be your date for this one. I didn't bring evening clothes, though. Didn't think I would need to dress up that much. I suppose I could..."

Carly giggled, unable to help herself. "Trust me, Alex. You won't need a tux. Jeans and boots will be the standard attire for the evening. It's a western theme party. I think you're going to find that a charity dance in Seventy-Six, Arkansas, is very different from one in Boston, Massachusetts."

"Since the ones in Boston usually bore me to my toenails, that sounds like a good thing."

"We'll see if you still feel that way this evening.

Would you like me to pick you up, or would you rather meet at the community center?''

''This is a date. I'll pick *you* up,'' he said firmly.

She lifted an eyebrow. ''The old-fashioned type, are you?''

He grinned. ''Only when it suits me.''

He kissed her again, thoroughly enough to make her pulse race alarmingly. And then he stepped back. ''I won't keep you any longer. I'll see you this evening.''

''Seven o'clock,'' she remembered to tell him, having to force her well-kissed lips to form the words clearly.

''I'll count the minutes,'' he quipped. The smile he shot over his shoulder as he made his way out left her standing in the middle of the room with her heart thudding against her chest and her breath caught somewhere in her throat.

The man was dangerous.

But, oh, could he kiss!

Alex was standing outside Carly's door exactly at seven. He hadn't brought western clothing with him, so he'd chosen to wear a gray sport coat over a white shirt and jeans, with boots and a whimsical Mickey Mouse tie that a group of nurses had given him in honor of his birthday. They'd probably considered it a joke, but Alex liked it. It made him smile.

His smile froze when Carly opened the door.

She'd pinned her dark blond hair up into a loose knot with a few soft tendrils escaping around her face, practically begging Alex to brush them back. She wore a white satin shirt with red trim and a short denim skirt that hugged her hips and left her legs bare from midthigh down to her red, tooled-leather western boots. A small pager was clipped discreetly to her red leather belt, the only reminder of her profession.

Alex had seen some of the world's most beautiful women dressed in diamonds and sequins, slinky, revealing dresses straight from Paris fashion runways, scraps of silk that had probably cost more than Carly earned in a year. And not one of those stunning women had shattered his ability to speak coherently simply by appearing in a doorway.

She gave him a smile that destroyed the remainder of his working brain cells. "Hello, Alex. I hope you're ready for this."

As a matter of fact, he hadn't been prepared for this at all. How could he have known that he would arrive in what many of his acquaintances would consider the middle of nowhere, only to find a woman who figuratively knocked him flat on his backside?

In response to his extended silence, Carly looked up at him inquiringly. "Alex?"

"I, uh—" He cleared his throat, trying to clear his mind at the same time. "You look...great."

She wrinkled her nose, a gesture Alex found incredibly appealing. "Thank you. I was going to wear jeans, but Granny insisted I should wear a skirt."

"On behalf of every man who will see you tonight, let me just say, 'Thank you, Granny,'" Alex murmured, looking down at Carly's long, beautiful legs and resenting every other man who would view them.

Carly laughed softly, ruefully. "Do you *try* to embarrass me, or does it just come naturally to you?"

He lifted his eyes to hers again, his smile wry. "Do you *try* to captivate me, or does it just come naturally to you?"

Her cheeks darkened. "Okay, you win. I'm embarrassed."

He reached out to run a thumb across her lower lip. "And I'm captivated. I'd call it a tie."

Her lip trembled slightly beneath his touch, tempting him almost overwhelmingly to taste her again. She pulled back before he could follow through on the impulse.

"I'll get my purse," she said, looking flustered. "Would you like to come in and say hello to my grandmother before we leave?"

Alex stepped through the door. "Betty isn't going to the dance?"

"No. She said these things get too loud and boisterous for her. She'd rather stay home and read or watch television."

Betty was already settled on the couch, a crocheted afghan draped around her, a cup of tea beside her, a book in her lap and an old movie just beginning on the television. She looked perfectly content to remain just that way, though she seemed delighted that Carly and Alex had other plans.

"I hope you have a wonderful time," she said, beaming at Alex.

"I'm sure we will."

"Don't you let anyone bother you with pesky questions, you hear? We're a nosy bunch, but well-intentioned, for the most part."

Alex nodded. "I can handle it."

Betty chuckled. "I imagine you can."

And then she looked at Carly, and her smile dimmed a bit. "I hope Ronnie Mayo and his cronies don't cause any trouble tonight."

Carly grimaced. "Ronnie knows he's walking a

fine line with the law these days. Officer Barton is just waiting for an excuse to lock him up.''

''Local troublemaker?'' Alex asked, knowing the type.

''A real jerk. Seems like I'm always stitching up someone who got on Ronnie's bad side...not that he has a good side,'' Carly answered in distaste.

Betty nodded. ''Thirty-five years old and he's never outgrown swaggering adolescence. He gives Carly a particularly hard time, I'm afraid. He made a real pest of himself when she first moved here, and he has resented ever since that she wouldn't have anything to do with him.''

Alex's eyes narrowed. ''He won't be bothering her tonight.''

''Trust me, I can deal with Ronnie Mayo,'' Carly said dryly. ''I've been doing so for a long time.''

She wouldn't be dealing with the jerk tonight. Alex might have been amused at his uncharacteristically aggressive surge of testosterone if he hadn't been so annoyed at the thought of some guy causing Carly distress.

''Anyway, let's not borrow trouble,'' Carly continued. ''Ronnie might not even show up tonight. Are you ready to go, Alex?''

He nodded. ''You're sure you don't want to go with us, Betty?''

She smiled, obviously pleased that he'd asked. ''Thank you, dear, but I'm quite comfortable where I am. You two kids have a wonderful time, you hear? And drive carefully.''

Alex chuckled. It had been a while since anyone had called him a kid.

Making a face at her grandmother, Carly tucked her

red leather purse beneath her arm and turned for the door. "We'd better go before she pulls out the camera."

Betty's eyes lit up. "I hadn't even thought of that. You two would make such a lovely picture, all dressed up for your party. Love your tie, Alex. Carly, why don't you..."

"Good night, Granny. Don't wait up." Carly all but dragged Alex to the front door. Grinning, he waved goodbye to Betty before allowing himself to be towed outside.

Alex walked Carly to the passenger side of his car and opened the door, gave her a hand in, then closed the door for her. The old-fashioned courtesy was a novelty for her. It had been a long time since a man had made a fuss over taking her out.

Actually, it had been a long time since she'd been out with a man, she reflected, trying to remember the last real date she'd had. Going to the movies with Bob didn't count, since they had never even aspired to be more than just friends.

She glanced at Alex as he slid behind the wheel. She wasn't sure she could ever feel as comfortable and breezy with Alex as she did with most of the other men she knew. The strong attraction she felt every time she looked at him, the way she reacted to his every smile and touch, the fantasies that popped into her head every time he gazed into her eyes...all added up to the potential for a great deal more than casual friendship.

The potential for heartache, if she didn't start being more careful.

"Where is the community center?" Alex asked as he backed out of the driveway.

"On the other side of town. It'll only take us fifteen minutes or so to get there."

"Do we have to be right on time?"

"No. It's a drop-in sort of thing, from seven until ten."

"Good. Let's take the long way and talk."

She moistened her lips. "What would you like to talk about?"

"You."

Carly made a face. "That shouldn't take long. What do you want to know?"

"Everything," Alex answered simply. "When and why you decided to become a doctor. Where you went to school. How you ended up here. What your plans are for the future. What the chances are that you'll go back to my cabin with me after the dance."

He slipped that in so smoothly that Carly almost missed it. She frowned. "Alex..."

"Okay, forget that last one—for now. Answer the others."

"Um..." She could hardly remember what else he wanted to know.

He made it easier for her. "When did you know you wanted to be a doctor?"

"That's sort of a complicated story."

He settled comfortably into his seat and drove more slowly. "I'd like to hear it."

She looked out the window at the familiar scenery, the community where she'd made her home for the past five years. But she was seeing another rural area, in a different part of the state.

"I grew up in Leslie, Arkansas, which isn't all that far from here," she said. "It's a poor town—particularly so when I was growing up there. My father was a self-taught mechanic. He worked on the old cars and trucks our neighbors drove and took whatever they could afford to pay him in return. Mom stayed at home to raise my three brothers and me. We lived in a little three-bedroom house heated in the winter by a woodstove and cooled in the summer by window fans. My brothers and I ran around barefoot all summer, wearing clothes Mama bought at the thrift store or at garage sales. We ate a lot of beans and corn bread, and whatever fish and game Daddy brought home when he had time to hunt or fish. We were better off than many of our neighbors—we never had to rely on the government to help feed us—but we were what most people would consider poor.''

She didn't look at Alex as she spoke, didn't try to gauge his reaction to her background, which she knew must be very different from his own. ''My father,'' she continued, ''never finished high school. It was very important to him for his children to do so. Every night after dinner we all sat around the kitchen table doing our homework and studying for tests, with Daddy standing over us to make sure we didn't slack off. He was at every teacher-parent conference, every PTA meeting, every school program. Every spare penny he earned went straight into our college funds.''

''He wanted to prepare you for your future. That's what makes a good father, isn't it?''

''He was the best,'' she agreed with a misty smile. ''His family was everything to him. He loved us without reservation. He made us believe that there was nothing we couldn't do.''

''It sounds like your family was rich in everything that counted.''

She looked at him then, touched by his words and by the faint wistfulness in his voice. "Yes. We were."

"What happened to him?" he asked gently, perceptively.

Carly's throat tightened. "Daddy took wonderful care of everyone but himself. He died of cancer when I was fourteen. If he had taken off work to go to the doctor when he first started noticing problems, there's a chance he might have been treated. As it was, he waited too late. He lasted only a few months after the cancer was diagnosed."

Alex was silent for a moment, as if he knew there was little he could say in the face of her old, but still painful, grief. And then he asked quietly, "Is that when you decided to become a doctor?"

"Perhaps," she answered with a slight shrug. "I don't remember a specific moment. It just seemed a natural path for me to follow when I went to college on a full academic scholarship."

"Which college?"

"The University of Arkansas at Fayetteville. Followed by the U of A Medical School in Little Rock. I did my internship and residency in Little Rock, but I knew all along I wanted to work in a rural area. I took over this clinic five years ago when the doctor who'd practiced here for more than forty years retired."

"And is that how long you plan to practice here?"

"I have no plans to move anytime soon," she replied. "I feel needed here. Not many medical school graduates are interested in coming to an area where the hours are long and the pay is low compared to more urban practices. For that matter, fewer young doctors are interested in primary care as opposed to specialty practices.''

''That's true. Primary care doesn't have the perceived glamour of specialized medicine,'' Alex mused. ''Many bright young medical students aren't interested in dispensing antibiotics or treating routine colds and flu.''

''Primary care is as important as any specialty,'' Carly argued, a bit offended by his description of her work. ''Yes, I deal mostly with minor health problems. But I'm the first defense against catastrophic illness for many of the families around here. I deliver their babies, treat their sniffles and their injuries, monitor their blood pressure and cholesterol. I'm the one who sends them to one of those specialists when necessary, the one who knows when and where to guide them. If my father had had a family practitioner he'd trusted and consulted, he might still be alive.''

Alex nodded toward a large, metal-sided building ahead, its parking lot filled to overflowing. ''Is that the community center?''

''Yes. Looks like a good turnout. We'll probably have to park on the roadside and walk.''

He pulled over to park behind a rust-spotted van. ''How's this?''

''Fine. Alex, are you sure you want to do this? It's going to be crowded and noisy, and the locals are likely to ask you all kinds of personal questions. A visitor is always cause for gossip around here.''

''Does gossip concern you?''

She shook her head. ''No, but...''

His smile took her voice away. ''Then let's give them something to talk about, shall we?'' he murmured, and tugged her to him for a hard, quick kiss before he opened his door and climbed out of the car.

Carly waited until Alex walked around to open her door before she even tried to get out. It took her that long to recover the breath Alex had stolen with his kiss.

It was going to be a very interesting evening. She was finding it hard to imagine how it would all end. Would Alex ask her again to accompany him to his cabin when the dance ended?

And if he did, would she answer with her head—or with her heart?

Eight

There were a great many interesting things about the charity dance, but Alex found Carly's interaction with the other guests the most interesting of all. There must have been two hundred people in the community center, and Carly seemed to know them all.

''Good evening, Pearl,'' she greeted the woman who stood at the door taking tickets. ''How are you?''

''Doing real good, Dr. Fletcher.'' The fiftyish woman wore what appeared to be square-dance clothing—a ruffled red-and-white gingham shirt and a full denim skirt held straight out by underlying layers of net. Her frosted hair was sprayed almost as stiff as her petticoats. ''My knees aren't bothering me near as much as they did before, thanks to that new medicine you gave me.''

''Glad to hear it. How's Tricia? Is she ready to move back home yet?''

Pearl laughed. ''Her daddy would sure like that, but she's real happy at that college. She's got a lot of new friends and she's making straight A's so far. She sure is grateful to you for helping her get that scholarship.''

Carly waved a hand, the gesture self-deprecating. ''All I did was write a letter of recommendation. And every word I wrote was true. Tricia earned that scholarship by working so hard and making such good grades in high school.''

Pearl's attention had already turned to the man at Carly's side. ''Who's this?''

''Pearl McMahon, this is Alex Keating. He's visiting from Boston.''

There wasn't time for more than perfunctory greetings, since a line was beginning to form behind them. Pearl waved Carly and Alex into the crowded room, which was decorated with bales of hay, black cardboard cowboy silhouettes taped to the walls and strings of red lights shaped like chili peppers. At one end of the room was a small stage, decorated in the same cowboy theme, on which a country-and-western band performed with more volume and enthusiasm than talent. A cash bar was set up at the other end of the room, manned by bartenders in white shirts with red garters on their sleeves. Overhead, a large banner reminded the guests that the proceeds of the event would benefit the volunteer fire department.

''Hey, Doc,'' someone shouted over the noise. ''How's it going?''

''Fine, Bill. Is Elsie with you tonight?''

''Yeah, she's here somewhere. She's feeling a lot better since you gave her that antibiotic.''

''Glad to hear it.''

''Dr. Fletcher!'' A teenage girl with a mild case of acne and a bad case of giggles hitched at the straps of her too large overalls as she skidded to a stop in front of Carly. ''I got an A on my science report. Thanks for your help.''

''You're welcome, Brenda. You can just drop those books by my office whenever you get a chance, okay?''

"I'll bring them back tomorrow," Brenda promised. She looked at Alex from beneath long, darkened lashes and giggled again. "Is this your boyfriend, Dr. Fletcher?"

"This," Carly answered quickly as Alex broke into a grin, "is Mr. Keating. He's a friend."

"Hi, Mr. Keating. Cool tie."

"Thank you," Alex replied, deepening his smile until Brenda blushed and giggled again.

"Stop that," Carly muttered the moment Brenda disappeared into the crowd.

He lifted an eyebrow. "Stop what?"

"That sexy smile. The women around here aren't used to it. You want to cause a riot or something?"

Alex laughed. "Now you're trying to embarrass *me*, right?"

She sighed deeply. "As if I could." She shook her head, then asked almost challengingly, "Do they two-step in Boston?"

"Some of us do," he answered, sliding an arm around her waist to accompany her to the busy dance floor as the band launched into an old country-swing number.

He was grateful now that a former girlfriend had insisted on dragging him to several country-dance classes. She'd hoped to find a hobby that would give them more of a common bond. It had turned out that she hated country dancing, while Alex enjoyed it. They'd broken up after only half a dozen lessons, and Alex had missed the dancing more than his partner.

He wasn't at all sure that would have been the case had Carly Fletcher been the one to introduce him to the pleasures of country dancing. He felt a jolt of desire hit him when she turned to move into his arms, and he had to remind himself that they were surrounded by her friends, neighbors and patients. He would have to behave himself and hold her decorously—though what he really wanted to do was to pull her so tightly against him that a wisp of smoke couldn't pass between them.

He thought he saw a gleam of answering awareness in Carly's dark eyes when she gazed up at him. His fingers twitched at her side but remained in place as he resisted the urge to shape the curve of her denim-covered hip with his palm. Determined not to make a complete fool of himself, he began to move with the rhythm of the music, and Carly followed as if they'd been dancing together for years.

Even on the dance floor, Carly was barraged with greetings and comments. She answered each one, displaying a phenomenal memory for names and faces and little personal details that probably made each of her acquaintances feel special to her.

Alex wasn't at all sure he would recognize two out of five of the patients he'd treated during the past ten years, especially outside the clinical setting. He'd saved lives—hundreds of them—and pioneered techniques that had been refined and utilized all over the country. But somewhere along the way, his patients had become cases to him rather than individuals. Numbers. Challenges.

To Carly, they were friends. Neighbors. Family.

Alex's patients spoke to him with respect. Awe, even.

Carly's patients didn't seem to regard her with a distant admiration. They genuinely liked her. Some of them even loved her.

He knew she'd thought he was criticizing her earlier when he'd made comments about her primary care practice. She couldn't have been more wrong. Alex admired Carly a great deal. Both professionally and personally.

Carly seemed to suddenly become aware of the silence between them. "You dance very well."

"You sound surprised."

"I just didn't think country dancing would be very big in Boston."

"You've never been there, have you?"

Carly made a face. "I haven't traveled much," she admitted. "I was supposed to go to Boston for a medical convention three years ago, but the doctor who was going to fill in for me here had a family emergency and my plans fell through."

Alex had been the keynote speaker at a medical convention in Boston three years ago. If Carly had attended, would they have met then? And if they had, would Alex have fallen as hard and as fast as he had here? Or would he have been so caught up with his own importance and reputation that he would have written her off as a simple country doctor who shared nothing in common with him?

He suspected he would have looked into Carly's dark eyes and been lost, just as he had the day he'd been hauled into her office, bleeding and dazed. He really should tell her who he was. What he did. There was no good reason for his continued silence on the subject. Except for his deep-seated worry that the truth would prove more of an obstacle between them than a common bond.

"Maybe you'll get another chance to visit Boston," he said instead. "I'd like to show you around."

Carly murmured something noncommittal and

smiled at someone over Alex's shoulder. And he knew she was thinking that the odds of him showing her around Boston were slim at best.

Alex tried to imagine Carly at one of the charity affairs he was so often compelled to attend. He had no doubt that she would fit in, that she would be the most beautiful woman in the room, at least in his eyes. But would she glow with the same simple enjoyment there that he saw in her now, here among her friends?

Someone else called her name and Carly lifted her hand from Alex's shoulder to wave, her smile beaming. She loved these people. She loved this place. Would Alex ever see her again after he returned to Boston next week?

Fortunately, he was distracted from that depressing question when a heavy hand clapped him on the shoulder the moment the dance ended. "Well, hey, there. You're sure looking a lot better than you did last time I saw you. See you've still got that bruise on your head, though. Still hurt?"

Recognizing Burle, the big man who'd rescued him from the river on Thursday, Alex smiled. "No, it's fine. And now that I can speak coherently again, I'd like to thank you for what you and your friend did for me last week."

Burle waved off his thanks. "No big deal. Anyone woulda done it. Hey, Doc," he added, glancing at Carly. "How you doing?"

"Fine, thank you, Burle. How's Millie?"

"She's over there in the corner running her mouth to Camilla Newberry about something…or someone. Nothing those women like better than a good gossip. I was real surprised to see you come in with Alex here. Did you decide to keep him once you patched him up?''

Burle laughed heartily at his own joke. Alex mused that Burle's wife wasn't the only one who enjoyed a ''good gossip.'' Carly deflected the teasing easily enough, and then another song began, giving them the excuse to start dancing again.

After the third dance, Carly and Alex took a break and moved toward the bar. Alex ordered a glass of wine, Carly a diet cola. There weren't any empty folding chairs along the edges of the dance floor, so they leaned against a wall as they sipped their drinks and watched the dancers.

''The band is pretty good, isn't it?'' Carly asked, making conversation.

Alex lifted an eyebrow and settled for a neutral murmur.

Carly laughed. ''Okay, so I'm comparing them to the last band that played here. Trust me, this group is wonderful next to them.''

Before Alex could reply, a very pregnant young woman approached them, wearing a determined look on her face and towing an embarrassed-looking young man by his hand.

''Dr. Fletcher, would you please tell Andy that it's okay for me to dance?'' the woman demanded in an exasperated tone. ''He acts like I'm going to break or something.''

Smiling, Carly glanced down at her patient's very large middle. ''I'd take it easy if I were you, Nancy. The baby's due in less than a month.''

''I'm not planning on doing anything fancy. Just a little slow dancing.''

The baby's father snorted. "Like I could get close enough to you to slow dance with you."

Nancy glared at him. "We could manage," she insisted. "I love to dance, and who knows when I'm going to get another chance? Tell him it's okay, Dr. Fletcher."

Carly took pity on her. "Just don't overdo it, Nancy. One or two dances, then get off your feet for a break, okay?"

Nancy nodded eagerly. "Come on, Andy. We'll ask them to play our song."

"Sucker," Alex murmured into Carly's ear.

She laughed. "Nancy's healthy as a horse. It won't hurt her to move around on the dance floor a little, as long as she's careful. And Andy will make sure of that."

"What if the band doesn't know their song?"

"Then they'd better learn it. Nancy has a way of getting what she wants."

"Will you deliver her baby?"

Carly nodded. "The county hospital is a twenty-minute drive away. It's small and underfunded, but adequate for routine deliveries and general health care. Serious cases are transferred to Harrison or Little Rock here in the state, or to Springfield, Missouri, depending on circumstances."

"How many doctors are on staff at the county hospital?"

"Not nearly enough," she replied somberly. "But we get by."

"By being on call twenty-four hours a day, seven days a week?"

"Pretty much," she admitted. "I'm hoping to take on a partner within the next year, which will give me a little more free time. We've had quite a few Spanish-speaking residents move into the area recently to work at the plants in surrounding towns, and I'd like to find someone who's fluent in Spanish. My own is barely adequate."

Alex had minored in Spanish in college and had spent several summers in Latin America as part of a volunteer program his father had recommended, mostly because it looked good on a résumé. Alex had come back with an impressive command of the language and a commitment to raising money for the struggling medical clinics he'd worked with there. Because of his efforts in Boston, thousands of dollars had been put to good use in those poor countries, though Alex had never gone back to visit.

He realized now that he'd given little thought to the struggling medical clinics in his own country. He'd donated his services on many occasions to patients who couldn't afford him, but he'd always had plenty of money to make up the difference. Philanthropy came relatively easily to the wealthy.

Had he ever truly sacrificed for his patients, given himself as selflessly and generously as Carly did all the time? He knew the answer was no. Which made him even more reluctant to confess to Carly that he and she shared the same profession in such dramatically different ways.

He set his empty glass on a tray left on a bale of hay for that purpose. "Let's dance."

He wanted his hands on Carly again.

The band was playing a slow number, so slow that most of the couples on the dance floor were doing little more than swaying in place. Which suited Alex just fine.

He knew they were being watched. Whispered and speculated about. But he didn't care. It felt so good to hold her. And if the attention they drew bothered Carly, she didn't let it show when she rested her head against Alex's shoulder and swayed with him.

It didn't take long for Alex to realize that he'd better start making conversation—fast—to distract himself from the feel of Carly in his arms, before he thoroughly embarrassed himself.

"I thought I would see Debbie and Bob here this evening," he murmured, glancing over Carly's head and not seeing either among the crowd.

"Bob works with the youth group at his church on Monday nights," Carly explained. "They meet for pizza or hot dogs and Bible study. And Debbie said she just wasn't interested in coming tonight."

"I had lunch with Debbie yesterday."

"Yes, I heard," Carly said.

Alex should have known that the town gossips would have shared that tidbit with Carly. He wondered what she'd thought upon hearing it.

"We ran into each other by accident at her aunt and uncle's restaurant," he explained. "Since we were both there alone, we decided to share a table."

"Did you have a nice visit?" Carly asked, her voice studiously casual.

"Yes. Your nurse is a very...interesting woman."

"She can be difficult to understand at times. She tends to put people's backs up with her bluntness and her dry sense of humor. Still, I'm very fond of her."

"Do you think she'll ever give Bob a chance?"

Carly sighed. "I don't think so. She's dead set against getting involved with a minister...even though I think she likes him very much."

"She's in love with him."

Carly looked up at him with a startled expression. "Debbie told you that?"

He shook his head. "Not in so many words."

"Oh. Well then..."

"She's in love with him. And he loves her. Seems like there would be something they could do to get past their problems."

Carly tilted her head and studied Alex's face so intently that he was tempted to look away. "I never would have pegged you as a matchmaker," she said after a moment.

He made a face. "I'm not usually. In fact, it's something I've always made it a practice to avoid. It's just...well, I like your friends. It seems a shame that they're both so unhappy."

Carly's eyes narrowed and her hand twitched in his. And then she shook her head and spoke with what might have been resignation. "You're starting to scare me, Alex Keating."

He didn't ask her to explain. Somehow he knew exactly what she meant. "Good," he murmured, drawing her just a little closer. "Because you terrify me."

"The sensible thing," she murmured, "would be for us to stay far away from each other."

"Probably," he agreed, his chest tightening at the thought. "But I don't think that's going to happen, do you?"

He held his breath while she considered her answer. After a moment, she gave a faint smile. "Remember that question you asked me earlier?"

"Which one?"

"You asked what the chances were that I would

go back to your cabin with you after the dance.'' She kept her voice low, meant for him alone. ''I would say they're getting better all the time.''

Alex had to remind himself that they weren't alone. That this wasn't the time to pull her closer and show her exactly what she did to him when she looked up with that deep glow of warmth in her chocolate brown eyes. But later…well, the chances were getting better all the time.

''How much longer do you think we should stay?'' he asked, hearing the husky edge to his voice.

The song ended and Carly stepped back. ''I think we can leave now,'' she said with a smile that wasn't quite steady.

''Hey, you can't leave yet, Doc. You ain't danced with me yet.''

Carly stiffened, and her smile faded.

Alex turned to look at the man who'd spoken. Late thirties, maybe. Dark hair, stringy in front and tied into a shoulder-length ponytail in back. A fuzz of beard spotting his cheeks and chin. A too tight olive T-shirt stretched over weight-trained muscles and was tucked into loose, camouflage-print pants worn with thick-soled boots. He reeked of beer, most of which he'd probably consumed before he'd entered the community center, since there was a two-drink maximum at the cash bar.

The guy probably thought he looked like a young Sylvester Stallone or some other Hollywood hero. Alex thought he looked ridiculous.

''Sorry, Ronnie. We were just leaving.'' Carly's voice was cool.

Alex remembered the name. Ronnie Mayo. The guy who'd been giving Carly trouble.

Mayo gave Alex an openly derisive once-over. "Who's this?"

Carly made a perfunctory introduction. "Ronnie Mayo, this is Alex Keating."

"You ain't from around here, are you, Keating?"

"No. I'm only visiting."

Mayo lifted his eyebrows. "Yeah? Where from?"

"Boston. Now, if you'll excuse us, we were just..."

But Mayo wasn't one to take a hint. "Boston, huh? Well, ain't that special." He curled one side of his upper lip into what he probably considered a cool sneer, but which only made him look not particularly bright. "I figured you must have money or something. The doc here thinks she's too good for the local boys who work for a living."

Carly deliberately turned her back on the other man, looking up at Alex with anger-brightened eyes. "Shall we go?"

Alex was both relieved and somewhat surprised that Mayo didn't try to detain them further as they turned toward the door. Apparently, the guy was all talk.

When they *were* detained, it was for a reason that was all too familiar to any doctor in a social situation. A request for free medical advice.

"The toenail on my big toe on my right foot is all red and puffy," a woman complained in a low voice, after catching Carly's arm and greeting her with the familiarity of longtime acquaintances. "It's real sore. What can I do about it?"

"Sounds like you have an ingrown toenail," Carly replied, her tone warmer now than it had been when she'd spoken to Mayo.

"We could go into the rest room and you could look at it for me," the woman suggested.

Carly smiled, and Alex had to admire her patience. "I don't think that's necessary this evening," she said. "Soak your foot in warm water and Epsom salt tonight, and call my office tomorrow for an antibiotic prescription. Take that for a few days to clear up the infection, and then I'll look at your toe to see what else we need to do to it."

The woman asked a few more questions, obviously reluctant to let Carly get away while she had her attention. And then someone else came up to talk, followed by yet another of Carly's friends. It was another fifteen minutes before Alex and Carly could make their escape.

Alex let out a deep breath when they stepped outside. Matching their steps, they began the long walk across the parking lot toward the road where Alex had parked.

"I was beginning to think you were going to have to set up a makeshift clinic right there in the community center."

Carly laughed softly, ruefully. "One of the disadvantages of dating a doctor," she admitted. "That and the possibility that my pager could start beeping at any minute."

He knew all too well the disadvantages of dating a doctor. Again, Alex felt a ripple of guilt that he hadn't exactly been honest with Carly about himself. He really should tell her the truth before this evening went any further.

"Carly..."

Two dark figures stepped in front of them just as they left the parking lot.

Alex swallowed a groan when he recognized Ronnie Mayo. The guy with him was obviously another bodybuilder, muscles bulging out of a jersey bearing the markings of a pro football team. Both of them looked just drunk enough to be mean and stupid.

Alex really wasn't in the mood to have his face pounded. He glanced around for possible assistance, wondering why, with so many vehicles around, there weren't more people milling outside the community center.

"What do you want, Ronnie?" Carly asked, no intimidation apparent in her expression.

"We just wanted to welcome your friend here to our community." Mayo's words were a bit more slurred than they'd been less than twenty minutes earlier.

"Consider him welcomed. Now move out of the way, please. We'd like to leave."

"Your friend don't talk for himself?" Mayo reached out and flicked the end of Alex's tie. "Nice tie. Mickey Mouse, ain't it?"

Alex stepped to one side, his hand at Carly's waist. He was determined not to allow these jerks to provoke him. He hoped they would back down if Carly and he both ignored them. Alex didn't particularly care what they said or thought about him; he had no intention of fighting them.

They made it a couple of yards away. And perhaps Mayo would have let them go if his alcohol-encouraged friend hadn't decided to press the issue.

"You going to let him just walk off like that without saying nothin'?" the guy demanded of Mayo. "That's damn rude, ain't it? He thinks he's too good to talk to us."

"Hey, Boston," Mayo called, goaded into further action. "Is Bud right? You think you're better than us?"

"Just keep walking," Alex advised Carly when she seemed prepared to respond.

She bit her lip and nodded, staying close to his side as they took another few steps toward Alex's car.

And then a heavy hand fell on Alex's shoulder. He sighed deeply.

Damn it, he thought, even as he was jerked around. He'd really hoped to avoid this.

Mayo's first blow caught Alex squarely on the chin.

Nine

Carly watched Alex as he drove with his right hand and fingered his jaw with his left. "Is it sore?"

His left hand joined his right on the steering wheel. "No."

"I'm really sorry, Alex. I've always known Ronnie Mayo was a jerk, but I never expected anything like that."

"Don't apologize for him. You did nothing to provoke him."

"You're sure you're okay? You haven't said much since Ronnie and Bud were hauled off."

"I'm fine. I just don't like fighting."

For someone who didn't like fighting, Alex had been amazingly good at it. Ronnie and Bud had been almost comically astonished that the Bostonian with the Mickey Mouse tie had put them facedown in the dirt with only a few well-placed blows. The initial blow to the chin was the only one that had landed on Alex.

The skirmish hadn't lasted long. Realizing what was happening, several men from the dance had run over to help Alex out only moments after Ronnie took the first swing. By the time help arrived, Alex had already effectively taken care of both Ronnie and Bud. Carly suspected that by tomorrow, Alex would be a local hero, especially once the gossips got through exaggerating the circumstances.

"Did you perhaps do any boxing in college?"

"Yes."

"You must have been pretty good at it."

He nodded. "My father wanted me to train for the Olympics."

"Were you that good?"

"Maybe. But I had better uses for my hands. And for my face," he added wryly.

She sensed that Alex was slowly beginning to relax. Though the ugly incident had spoiled the good mood in which they'd left the dance, she could see the lines of tension easing around his mouth. She reached out to rest a hand lightly on his right forearm, feeling the muscles still bunched beneath his clothing.

"I really am sorry," she said. "I hate that this happened when you were attending a community event. I wouldn't want you to get a bad impression of our area."

He shrugged. "We have jerks in Boston, too. Don't fret about it."

She slid her hand up his arm to his neck. "You're still very tense," she murmured. "What you need is a good massage."

A muscle jerked beneath her hand.

"Is that an offer?"

"Yes." To mask her sudden, renewed attack of nerves, she smiled. "I figure it's the least I can do after all you've been through."

Alex turned onto the gravel road that led to his cabin. "The very least," he agreed huskily.

Alex didn't immediately get out of the car after pulling into the driveway and killing the engine. He sat with his hands on the steering wheel, staring at the cabin through the windshield.

When he spoke, his voice was uninflected. "I think you should know," he said, "that there's no reason at all for you to be worried about going inside with me. I'm completely respectable, no criminal record, no health problems. I'm not married, engaged or otherwise committed. But if you have any reservations about going in—any at all—just say so, and I'll take you home. I'll understand."

Carly couldn't help smiling when he concluded his careful little speech. "This sounds a lot like the lecture you gave me when I took you home that first night. I'm not in the practice of taking strange men into my home, Alex, or of going into theirs. If I hadn't trusted you from the beginning, I never would have let you get anywhere near my grandmother...or me."

He looked at her then, his expression faintly puzzled. "Why do you trust me? You hardly even know me."

With a shrug meant to express her own bemusement, Carly replied, "Call it instinct."

He reached out to touch her cheek with his fingertips. "And have your instincts ever led you wrong?"

"Very rarely." She thought briefly of her one most notable mistake, but pushed that thought to the back of her mind. Maybe Alex, too, was a mistake, but he wasn't Linc. Carly didn't like to think she could be foolish enough to make the same mistake twice.

Alex leaned over to brush his lips across hers. "You aren't wrong this time, Carly," he murmured against her mouth.

She hoped not. But he didn't give her a chance to express whatever slight doubt she might have. He crushed her mouth beneath his, pressing her into her seat. Carly locked her arms around his neck and kissed him back, exactly the way she'd been wanting to since...

Since when? The first time she'd seen him, bruised, bloody, wet and dazed, but still insisting he was perfectly capable of taking care of himself? Later that same evening, when he'd gravely thanked her and her grandmother for taking him in? Or had it been when he'd blushed after Granny had brought out his birthday cake and led the guests in singing to him? Or maybe when he'd been so embarrassed about getting stuck in the cave, so anxious to keep Bob and Debbie from seeing him in that position?

Had it happened the first time he'd kissed her?

How long did it take to fall in love?

Alex pulled her even closer, his hands gliding over the slick satin of her blouse. She trembled as she thought of how good it would feel when there was nothing at all between them. Alex murmured something soothing into her mouth, then deepened the kiss still further, his tongue sweeping past her lips and teeth to plunge into her mouth and drive her even higher.

He couldn't know how long it had been since she'd done anything like this. How long since she'd wanted like this. Ached like this. Needed like this.

She placed her hands on his face, feeling the slight roughness of hours-old beard against her palms. She wanted to memorize the feel of him, the taste of him, the faint, spicy scent of him. She wanted to remember every detail of this night, every word he'd said, every dance they'd shared, every kiss, every touch.

No matter what happened, she wanted this night to

treasure in her memories. And she wanted Alex to remember it, too, after he'd returned to whatever life he led in Boston.

His hand slid up her back and buried itself in her hair, holding her head still for longer and deeper kisses. With kisses alone, he brought her close to the edge of insanity, so lost in him that she became oblivious to their surroundings. The cramped interior of the car didn't bother her, nor did the gearshift digging into her thigh.

They could be in a cave or in the honeymoon suite at the Plaza. It didn't matter. His kisses transported her. He lifted his mouth only enough to say her name.

She nibbled at his lower lip. "Mmm?"

"Let's go inside."

"Okay." She pulled his mouth to hers again.

An eternity later, he pulled away, gasping for breath. "Carly?"

She trailed her hand down the side of his face, shaping his firm jaw, running her thumb across his beautiful mouth. "Yes?"

She thought she heard him bite back a groan.

"I'm getting too old to do this in a car."

"You're doing just fine," she murmured, and kissed his chin.

He laughed roughly, caught her mouth with his for another quick kiss, then drew away. "Wouldn't you rather go inside?"

She reached for her door handle.

They met in front of the car. Alex cupped her face in his hands and kissed her in the moonlight. A light breeze off the river whispered around them, and unseen night creatures sang a seductive serenade. Carly slid her arms up Alex's chest and around his neck, deciding this was the most romantic moment she'd experienced in a very long time...if ever.

Alex finally broke the kiss and turned to walk with her toward the cabin. They stopped twice more on the path, turning what should have been a two-minute walk into nearly ten. It took another three or four minutes for Alex to find the key to the front door and then stop kissing Carly long enough to find the lock.

She didn't bother to look around once they were inside, nor did Alex stop to turn on a light. He led her straight to the bedroom, using only the illumination of moonlight streaming through uncurtained windows to guide their way.

"You can still stop this," he murmured, even as he drew her down to the bed.

"I could have stopped this anytime I wanted to," she reminded him. She pulled him closer. "I didn't want to."

He groaned and gathered her against his chest. "I didn't plan to meet you," he muttered between long, deep kisses. "But, damn, I'm glad I did."

And so was she, Carly reflected as she buried her fingers in his thick, dark hair. Being in love again was as exhilarating as it was terrifying. No matter what happened, she would not allow herself to regret this night. She cupped his face in her hands, brought his mouth down to hers. Whatever happened, she would not let Alex forget this night, either.

One by one, the buttons of her satin shirt opened beneath his fingers to reveal the scrap of lace she wore beneath. Had she subconsciously known how this evening would end when she'd chosen her sexiest underthings rather than the practical cotton she usually wore?

Or maybe it hadn't been all that subconscious.

"I'll need help getting out of these boots," she murmured, rubbing the inside of her foot against his leg.

His sudden grin was mischievous...and devastating. "I kind of like the boots. Maybe you should leave them on."

Though his smile had nearly destroyed her ability to speak coherently, she managed to reply, "I don't think so."

"Then allow me."

Alex slid his hands very slowly from her waist, down her hips, over her thigh and knee until he reached the top of her boot. Carly shivered, not at all sure she would survive his "help." He'd left a trail of fire everywhere he touched...and they hadn't even undressed yet.

One by one he removed her boots, stopping to stroke her soles and tickle her toes, taking so long that she thought she might have to help him or go crazy. How could she have imagined that he could turn removing a pair of boots into such an erotic act?

By the time he'd removed her blouse and skirt, impatience drove her, making her fingers clumsy as she fumbled with the knot of his tie and the buttons of his shirt. Fortunately, he'd already shrugged out of his jacket and pulled off his boots.

Finally, after what seemed like an eternity, the garments were out of the way, scattered in untidy piles on the floor. And Carly was free to explore the magnificence that had been hidden beneath Alex's clothing.

She'd already known that Alex had a beautiful face. Now she knew that he was beautiful all over.

She ran her hands appreciatively over his broad, lightly furred chest. Down the subtly muscled arms that had surprised Ronnie and Bud with their strength. Across his flat stomach. And then lower, until he gasped and reached for her hand.

"This is going to be over before we get started if you keep that up," he said, his voice both hoarse and rueful. "I haven't dated anyone in a while. I've been…busy."

"I haven't dated in a while, either," she admitted, both surprised and pleased by his confession. "For lack of both time and interest."

"I hear it's like riding a bicycle." He nuzzled into her throat, and she arched to better accommodate him. "We'll probably remember what to do."

Alex proved very quickly that he remembered exactly what to do—from taking care of protection to taking Carly to the edge of insanity.

They went over that edge together.

Alex cradled Carly against his chest, his eyes closed as he luxuriated in the moment. He could hear her breathing, still rapid but gradually slowing. He felt her heart pounding in her chest, keeping rhythm with his own. Her hair tumbled around her face, tickling his chin. Her skin was damp and warm against his.

He wanted to freeze this moment, make it last forever. And it was the first time ever that he'd felt that way after making love. Always before, he'd been anxious to either get out of the bed or make love again. He couldn't remember ever feeling so content just to hold a woman against his heart and savor being with her. Just to think about how very special she was.

Maybe it was because Carly was the first woman who had ever been this special to him. And that was something he was going to have to think about later, after this glow of gratification wore off.

"Alex?" Carly's voice was low, sleepy. Contented.

He wasn't sure he could form a complete sentence, so he settled for a murmur. "Mmm?"

"What time is it?"

"Does it matter?"

"I can't stay out all night. Granny would worry."

Alex sighed and squinted at the illuminated clock on the table behind Carly. "It's a little after ten."

"Mmm. We have some time, then." She snuggled more cozily into his shoulder.

Alex chuckled. "You sound like a teenager with a curfew."

Carly's soft laugh vibrated against his chest. "Do I? Sorry. It's just that I haven't had a true social life in so long. Granny's not used to me being out extremely late except for medical emergencies, and I usually let her know where I am."

Alex reached up to remove a strand of her hair from the corner of his mouth. "Why haven't you had a social life?" he asked, genuinely curious.

How could a beautiful, talented, intelligent, successful and sensual woman like Carly not be inundated with invitations from interested men?

"I go out with friends," she replied with a slight shrug. "Bob and Debbie. Another woman friend who's married and has two children and needs to get away from the kids once a month or so to see a movie or have dinner and talk."

"But you don't date?"

"Rarely. You saw the group at the community center tonight. Most of the men are married. The ones who aren't tend to be quite a bit older than I am, or too young."

"Or like Mayo and his pal?"

"There aren't many like him, thank goodness. But I've been asked out a few times by guys who quickly find out that dating a doctor is more trouble than they'd expected. I'm often paged away from social events, or cornered by patients, or too tired to stay out late. Or distracted by a patient's problems. I'm hardly the life of the party."

Alex knew all of those handicaps all too well. Carly had just effectively summed up the reasons he had always given for remaining unattached.

"You've never had a serious relationship?" he asked, hoping he wasn't being overly personal. This was something else that was new for him. He'd never particularly cared about a woman's romantic history before.

Carly hesitated so long that he decided he *had* overstepped his boundaries. He had just opened his mouth to apologize for his prying when she spoke.

"There was someone once. I met him when I was doing my residency in Little Rock. He was an internist, five years my senior. Except for my interest in practicing in a disadvantaged, rural area—which he didn't share at all—I thought we had quite a bit in common. It turned out that when it came to the most important things, we had very little in common. He had a serious problem with honesty."

Alex winced. "Er, what do you mean?"

"His idea of boosting his income was to fleece the Medicare system. It didn't bother him at all to overcharge for his services or to charge for services he never provided. He said everyone did it, and he derided me for speaking out against it. He called me sanctimonious and unrealistic and told me I would never get anywhere if I didn't learn to play the system. When I broke up with him and bought this clinic, he went around telling everyone what a fool I was to walk away from a promising future and settle for a backwater practice that would never make me wealthy."

Alex scowled. "How long did you know that guy?"

"I dated him for more than a year. I was naive," she added regretfully. "It took me that long to look beneath his charming and attractive surface and see what he really was."

Alex shook his head in disbelief. "He dated you for over a year and didn't know you better than that? I've only known you a few days and I know that you didn't become a doctor to become wealthy. And that you would never compromise your integrity for monetary profit."

Carly lifted her head to smile at him, her face glowing in the shadowy half light. "Thank you. That's the nicest thing anyone has said to me in a long time."

Alex knew it was time to come clean. Carly valued honesty, and he hadn't exactly been honest with her. He hadn't lied to her, he reminded himself quickly; he just hadn't volunteered the truth. He hoped she would appreciate the difference.

"There's something I should tell you about what I do in Boston."

Her smile faded. "Please tell me it doesn't involve fraud."

"Nothing like that," he assured her quickly.

Alex had never overcharged for any of his services, never taken a penny he hadn't earned. He reminded himself of the indigent patients he'd treated. He didn't intend to boast about those generous gestures to Carly, but it bolstered his courage to remind himself that he wasn't nearly as bad as the guy who'd hurt her before.

"I—"

A shrill, rapid beeping coming from somewhere on the floor sliced neatly through his words.

"Damn."

Carly gave him an apologetic look. "It's my pager."

"Yes, I know." He rolled out from under her, made a dive for the floor and sorted through the tangled garments until he found the noisy plastic box.

Carly took it with a murmured thanks, pressing a button to silence the beeping and illuminate the message area. Her brow shot up. "Looks like I have a baby to deliver."

Alex hazarded a guess. "The woman at the dance?"

She nodded. "Nancy. Her husband will probably blame me for this."

"Is it too early?"

"Not dangerously so." Carly slid off the bed and started separating her clothes from Alex's. "The due date's only three weeks away, and the baby's a good size now. They should both be fine. First babies are notoriously unpredictable."

Alex pulled on his shorts. "I'll drive you."

She pulled on her shirt and began to do up the buttons. "I'm sorry. You wanted to talk."

"We can talk later." He had no intention of trying

to explain himself when her thoughts were already focused on her upcoming delivery. There would be another opportunity for him to explain how well he knew the joys and heartaches of practicing medicine.

Carly insisted that Alex leave her at the hospital. "I'll find a way home," she assured him. "This will probably take hours."

He didn't want to leave her. He was tempted to stay and follow at her heels like a lovesick puppy. It was that disconcerting image that gave him the strength to remain behind the wheel of his car. He reached out to snag a hand behind her head and pull her to him for a lingering kiss.

"I'll call you," he said when he finally, reluctantly drew away.

She touched his face. "You'd better."

"I hope everything goes well in the delivery room."

"Thanks. So do I. Drive carefully, Alex. It's late, and you must be tired."

He smiled in response to her fussing. He rather liked it. "I still feel too good to be tired."

Her smile was quick and memory-warmed. "So do I. See you."

"See you." He watched as she climbed out of the car and hurried into the doctor's entrance of the little county hospital, her dark blond hair gleaming in the harsh artificial security lighting. Her hips swayed enticingly in the short denim skirt, her legs long and sleek in her red boots.

One sexy doctor, Alex thought with an appreciative exhale. And for a little while that evening, she'd been all his.

Ten

Carly hummed along with the piped-in music Tuesday afternoon as she left examining room two after writing a prescription for Jeremy Kennedy's ear infection and reassuring Jeremy's mother that the child would be just fine in a few days. It was pouring rain outside the clinic, but Carly felt as if she had sunshine bottled inside her.

Corny, she thought with a self-directed chuckle. But, oh, she felt good.

She was still basking in the exhilaration of being in love. Still refusing to think about the future. She'd gotten only a couple of hours' sleep after delivering Nancy and Andy's healthy, six-and-a-half-pound baby girl, but she wasn't sleepy. She was simply eager to wrap up her day so she could be with Alex again.

Wearing her usual frown, Debbie stepped out of an office into the hallway, almost colliding with Carly. "Oops. Sorry."

"No problem," Carly assured her with a smile.

Debbie regarded her suspiciously. "You sure have been smiling a lot today."

Carly shrugged. "What can I say? I'm in a good mood."

"Mmm. Wonder how much that has to do with your date last night."

Carly busied herself flipping through Jeremy's file and murmured something noncommittal.

Debbie followed Carly into her office. ''Ernestine Morgan just called. She said she saw you at the dance last night and you promised to prescribe an antibiotic for her ingrown toenail. She asked if you'd call it in to Price-Rite Pharmacy.''

Carly nodded. ''I've got a few other prescriptions to call in. I'll take care of them now.''

''Ernestine couldn't wait to tell me all the details about the dance. How you and that good-looking man danced all night and then left looking *very* cozy. And how Ronnie Mayo and one of his pals cornered y'all outside and your date beat the stuffing out of both of them.''

Carly set Jeremy's file on her desk and reached for a stack of telephone messages. ''You know how Ernestine exaggerates.''

''Mmm. She's not the only one who told me all about how friendly you and Alex looked last night. Some folks seem to be anticipating a catfight between you and me, since I had lunch with him Sunday and you took him to the dance Monday night.''

''Well, that just goes to show you that some folks need to get a life, doesn't it?'' Carly asked blandly.

''You know, of course, that my having lunch with Alex didn't mean a thing. We just happened to both be there at the same time. He's a nice guy, but not my type.''

''You don't have to explain anything to me, Debbie. It's none of my business who you have lunch with.''

Debbie smiled archly. ''When it comes to Alex, I think it's becoming your business. I'm not the only one who has noticed that the guy's tongue practically hangs out every time he's around you."

Carly's cheeks heated. "Honestly, Debbie. Don't you have work to do?"

"Mmm. You know what else Ernestine said?"

"I doubt that I want to hear it."

As deliberately oblivious as always, Debbie continued. "She said Alex looked so familiar to her, it bugged her all evening. She said she was sure she'd seen him someplace before, though she didn't think she'd ever actually met him."

"Ernestine is always seeing someone who reminds her of someone else," Carly reminded her nurse. "She tells me I look like Sandra Bullock with lighter hair. And she's always comparing you to that red-haired comic actress on Brooke Shields's sitcom. I suppose now she's decided Alex looks just like some good-looking, dark-haired actor."

Debbie shook her head. "She said she went home and thought about it and decided he didn't remind her of an actor. She thinks she saw him in a magazine article, but she couldn't remember whether it was in *People* or *Prominence Magazine.* You know how she loves her celebrity gossip magazines."

Carly looked up then. "Why would Alex have been featured in a celebrity magazine?"

Debbie shrugged. "I asked her that, of course, and she said she couldn't remember. She was going to spend this afternoon going through some of her hundreds of back issues, looking for him. She'll probably find some guy that vaguely resembles Alex, and she'll realize that it's nothing more than the similarities she's always finding in people."

Carly toyed with an ink pen, frowning thoughtfully.

"Carly?" Debbie seemed to read something into her employer's silence. "*Is* there some reason Alex would have been profiled in a magazine?"

"Not that I know of," Carly answered. Then added candidly, "But I really don't know much about Alex's life back in Boston. He doesn't talk about himself much."

"I noticed that. I don't even remember hearing what he does for a living. Has he told you?"

Carly shook her head, startled by the reminder of how little she really knew about the man she'd so recklessly given her heart to. "I've just assumed he's in business. He's never corrected me."

She thought of the conversation her pager had interrupted last night. Alex had been on the verge of telling her something, she remembered now. And she'd gotten the impression that he hadn't been sure she would like what he intended to say. The call to the hospital had distracted her, and it was only now that she remembered Alex's expression as he'd told her that he needed to talk to her about what he did in Boston.

Why was she suddenly uncomfortable about what he might have said? Surely she wasn't letting Debbie and Ernestine get to her with their paranoid fantasies?

Debbie's cinnamon brows drew together. "I gotta admit, I like the guy. He seems to have a good heart. He's been real nice to me. But…well, maybe you'd better be a little careful until you find out more about him, Carly. There could be a reason he doesn't want you to know more about him."

"And maybe Ernestine saw his face on a wanted poster in the post office," Carly retorted dryly.

Debbie didn't smile. "You laugh, but it could happen."

"Next time I see him, I'll ask if he's a criminal, okay? Will that make you feel better?"

Debbie's dour expression still didn't change. "Seems to me that it's about time you started asking him some questions."

Carly didn't argue with her any further. Not only because she had too many other things to do to waste more time, but also because she knew Debbie was right. It was time for Carly to start asking questions.

The first question should probably be what Alex envisioned for their future. Or if he envisioned a future for them at all.

The rain prevented Alex from fishing Tuesday afternoon. Restless in the cabin, alone with his memories of the night with Carly, he pulled on a denim jacket and dashed through the downpour to his car, not really knowing his destination.

He was tempted to drive to her clinic. Just to see her again, if only for a few moments. That devoted-puppy image popped back into his head, making him wince. Never in his life had he tagged around at a woman's heels, hoping for a few moments of her attention—not even as a teenager. He wasn't going to start at forty, he told himself flatly. That would be carrying this infatuation just a bit too far.

Infatuation. The word echoed for a few moments in his head. Was that what he felt for Carly? Was infatuation-at-first-sight a real phenomenon? Was it only lust, combined with his genuine respect for her? Or was it much, much more?

So he wouldn't go to the clinic. He would take Bob Calhoun up on his standing invitation, instead.

Alex didn't have many close friends in Boston; he tended to spend his spare time on the golf course with other doctors or on tennis courts with fellow members of his country club. He had one close friend from college—the one who'd introduced him to rock climbing—but Tony lived in another part of the country now, and Alex didn't see him as often as he might have liked. Something told Alex that, despite their obvious differences, he and Bob Calhoun could be friends.

The rain had let up considerably by the time Alex reached Bob's house. He noted that the sliding door to the workshop was cracked open, indicating Bob would probably be found inside. Alex wondered if Bob had been serious about his offer to let Alex play with his power tools. Might be interesting to make something out of wood.

Bob greeted Alex with every evidence of pleasure. "How's it going?" he asked, setting down the sander he'd been running over a length of sawn wood.

"The rain's put a damper on my fishing—pun intended." Alex frowned slightly as he studied Bob's face. "What's wrong?"

Bob mopped at his somewhat pale, sweat-glistened face with his right shirtsleeve. "Think I'm coming down with a bug," he admitted ruefully. "I haven't felt all that great since I woke up Sunday morning. And I'm worn-out after just a couple of hours of work today. Whatever it is, I hope it's not contagious. As glad as I am to see you, I'd hate to give you the flu on your vacation."

Considering everything else that had happened during Alex's vacation, a case of the flu sounded relatively innocuous. But he wasn't at all sure the flu was what ailed Bob.

"What are your symptoms?" he demanded, mentally cataloging Bob's poor color, audible shortness of breath and apparent clamminess.

Bob shrugged, typically male in his discomfort at discussing his weakness. "I feel unusually tired and I'm having some indigestion pains. It's no big deal. I just need an antibiotic or something. Carly will probably prescribe something for me, even though she isn't my usual doctor. I feel kind of funny about stripping down to my Skivvies in front of a friend," he added with a weak attempt at humor.

Alex didn't smile. An antibiotic wasn't what Bob needed, if Alex's well-trained instincts were correct. He reached for the other man's wrist, checking the pulse, finding it weak and thready.

Bob didn't resist, though he gave Alex a quizzical look. "Do you have any idea what you're doing?"

"Yes. Where are you experiencing pain?"

"It's sort of been moving around today," Bob answered with a casual shrug belied by the anxiety just becoming visible in his eyes. "My neck and chest, and between my shoulder blades mostly."

"Left arm?"

Bob swallowed hard. "A little," he admitted reluctantly. "It's probably just heartburn. Don't you think?"

He sounded as if he really wanted Alex to agree. Denial was a frequent reaction to myocardial infarction—especially in patients as young as Bob.

Alex palpated Bob's neck, then looked into his

eyes, first one, then the other. "Do you have a history of heart problems?"

"None," Bob answered confidently. "I'm as healthy as a horse."

"Family history?"

Bob's confidence faded visibly. "My grandfather and an uncle both died of heart attacks before they were fifty. But I had a full physical just a couple of years ago, and I got a clean bill. You're overreacting, Alex."

Alex kept his voice calm, steady. He didn't want to contribute to Bob's anxiety, which could well precipitate a crisis. "I'm taking you to the county hospital," he told him. "As you said, it's probably nothing serious, but I think you should be checked out."

"The hospital?" Bob shook his head. "I really don't think..."

"I'm afraid I'm not giving you an option," Alex said apologetically. "This isn't the flu, Bob. You need medical attention."

Bob studied Alex's face for a moment, then sighed, his expression resigned. "Why didn't you tell me you're a doctor?"

"It never came up."

Bob gave him a chiding look.

"We'll talk about it on the way to the hospital," Alex conceded.

Bob reached up to rub his chest, just left of center. "Whatever you think best," he said, his voice suddenly weaker, breathless.

Driven by a renewed sense of urgency, Alex took the other man's arm. "Let's go."

Carly had just stepped out of examining room three after a routine pap smear procedure when Debbie rushed up to her side. The expression on Debbie's usually placid face made Carly go cold. Debbie's voice was strained when she spoke. ''We just got a call from the hospital.''

Carly could tell that the news was bad—and that it was personal. ''Is it my grandmother?'' she whispered, almost afraid to hear Debbie's answer.

Debbie shook her head. ''It's Bob.''

Relief for her grandmother's sake warred with fear for her friend. Carly's first thought was that Bob had been injured while working in his shop. ''How badly is he hurt?''

''It's his heart.'' Debbie's eyes were dull, wounded. ''Myocardial infarction. By the time he reached the hospital, his condition was critical.''

''Oh, no.'' Carly could hardly believe it. Bob was the picture of a healthy, thirty-five-year-old man. He didn't smoke, wasn't overweight, got plenty of exercise, had normal blood pressure. But she knew full well that perfectly healthy-looking young adults sometimes died from heart failure. She'd encountered the tragic event more than once during her career.

She had never expected it to happen to Bob.

Carly dragged a hand through her hair, trying to think. Could she leave now? Did she have more patients waiting? Was there something she could do to facilitate Bob's care? ''How is he? What's being done for him?''

Debbie drew a long, ragged breath. ''Apparently, his care is being supervised by a highly respected east coast cardiologist. Karen Bishop, the nurse who called me, said the guy listed credentials that impressed the hell out of everyone over there.''

Carly frowned. What highly respected east coast cardiologist would be visiting their little county hospital? "Who is it?"

"His name is Dr. Robert Alexander Keating."

"Alex." Carly spoke in a stunned whisper.

"Yes."

"Did you know?"

Debbie shook her head. "Did you?"

"No." Carly didn't know what to say. What to think. How could she not have known? Why hadn't he said anything? As close as they had become during the brief time they'd known each other, why wouldn't he have told her that they shared the same profession? She was torn between hurt, anger and gratitude that he was taking care of her friend. She'd always suspected that Alex was the best at whatever he did. And it was entirely possible that Bob's life was in Alex's hands now.

"I have to go," Debbie said, her face suddenly anguished. "I have to..." Her voice broke.

"I'll take you," Carly promised, realizing for the first time the intensity of the feelings Debbie had been hiding for so long. Carly only hoped it wasn't too late for Debbie and Bob.

Alex had apparently given instructions for him to be notified when Carly and Debbie arrived at the hospital. He appeared in the waiting room less than fifteen minutes after they arrived.

Though he wore a blue chambray shirt, jeans and boots, the way he strode down the hallway made Carly wonder why she hadn't recognized him as a doctor the first time she'd seen him. He looked so right in the role. His calm, grave, professional expression was very similar to the one she characteristically assumed when approaching friends and family of critically ill patients.

He glanced first at her, a fleeting glimpse of apology in his eyes. And then he turned to Debbie, who'd rushed to him as soon as she saw him.

"How is he?" she demanded.

Alex took Debbie's hands. "He's being stabilized. He's been given aspirin and morphine and we're taking EKG readings now."

"I want to see him."

"He's pretty well out of it right now."

"I want to see him," she repeated stubbornly.

Carly was glad that Alex didn't try to detain her. Debbie knew emergency room procedure. She wouldn't get in the way.

Alex turned to Carly when Debbie left them. "She really loves the guy, doesn't she?"

"I believe she does. What happened, Alex?"

Alex hesitated, then sighed. "He scared the hell out of me," he admitted. "I went to see him, unannounced, and found him in his workshop, sweating, in pain, short of breath. He was in denial about his symptoms, trying to convince me—and himself—that it was heartburn or the flu. I thought I'd have to hog-tie him to get him into my car, but he agreed to come with me when I convinced him I knew what I was talking about."

"You told him you're a doctor."

"Yes."

Carly crossed her arms, tucking her hands into her elbows. "You didn't think that was something *I* might like to know?"

"I'm sorry." He shook his head. "That isn't enough, is it?"

"No."

"I'd like to try to explain why I didn't tell you—as soon as I figure it out myself—but I don't think this is the time or the place, do you?"

She wanted to be angry with him. He'd hurt her. She'd said she would never again fall for a man who wasn't honest with her. But when she looked at him, she saw the man she'd made love with only hours before. The man she'd fallen in love with sometime during the past few days. And she hoped she hadn't made another painful mistake.

She drew a deep breath. "You're a cardiologist."

"Yes." He studied her face as he spoke, obviously trying to read her emotions.

"R. A. Keating. I've heard of you, I think."

He shrugged. "I've published a few articles."

"Why didn't I put it together earlier?" She blamed herself almost as much as Alex for her ignorance. She'd been so busy lately that she'd had little time to keep up with her medical journals and professional networking. She thought she'd read something by or about Dr. R. A. Keating within recent months but couldn't for the life of her remember what it was.

"Considering the way we met, it isn't surprising you thought of me as a patient rather than a fellow doctor. And I certainly did nothing to change that first impression," Alex admitted. "I'm sorry, Carly. I didn't set out to deceive you. I was going to tell you last night, when your pager interrupted us."

She remembered that moment. Remembered that he'd told her there was something she needed to know about him. It helped somewhat that he'd wanted to tell her.

She put her hands into the pockets of the forest green blazer she wore with a matching pullover and a pair of khakis. "You're right. This isn't the time or place to discuss our personal problems. Tell me more about Bob. What was his condition on arrival?"

Following her lead, Alex switched into his professional mode. He spent the next few minutes describing Bob's condition, which he suspected was a previously undiagnosed congenital defect that would require surgery to correct.

Though it still startled Carly to hear Alex speaking in a language understood only by medical professionals, she followed his words closely, trying to maintain some emotional distance from this particular patient. It wasn't easy. This was Bob, her friend and neighbor, not just a patient with a list of serious symptoms.

She asked several questions, and Alex answered them thoroughly. And it made her feel a bit better to share this with him on both a personal and professional level.

She was really getting into trouble with Alex, she thought somewhere in the back of her mind. But she couldn't dwell on that right now. She had more pressing things to think about.

"Has anyone called Bob's family?" she asked.

"Not as far as I know. I asked someone to call you and Debbie, but I didn't know who else to notify."

Carly nodded. "I'll take care of it. His parents and siblings live in Missouri. And there are members of his congregation who'll want to be notified. I wish there was something definitive I could tell them."

"Until we know the extent of the damage, the only

thing you can say is that he's stable and being given the best of care."

Carly nodded. They were words she'd spoken too many times to count. She knew now that they were words that were much easier to say than to hear.

It was while Carly was in the hospital waiting room later that evening that she saw the magazine article. Alex had gone back to check on Bob, Debbie had been persuaded to leave for a short time to have something to eat, and Bob's family members were talking quietly among themselves on the other side of the waiting room. Restless and feeling rather useless since Alex was more qualified to take care of Bob than she was, Carly flipped idly through the weeks-old magazines provided in the waiting room, looking for anything that would distract her until Alex reappeared with an update.

She selected *Prominence Magazine* to glance through—a glossy, celebrity-filled publication full of social tidbits and fashion articles that held almost no relevance for the residents of little Seventy-Six, Arkansas, and the surrounding rural hills. Carly skimmed an article about a beautiful, thirty-something actress who had just married for the fourth time. She curled her lip at the outrageous garments featured in a famous designer's latest fashion show, trying to imagine the reaction if she appeared in any of them on the streets—or rather, the street—of Seventy-Six. She'd be laughed right out of town.

She turned another page and almost sneered at a bold, stylistic heading announcing "another candidate for the world's most eligible bachelors." And then her fingers froze on the page when she spotted the photograph that accompanied the article and the name printed beneath it.

Dr. Robert Alexander Keating.

Alex.

Eleven

Though Bob wasn't at all happy about it, Alex, Carly and the other staff at the county hospital agreed that he should be transferred to Little Rock. Alex engaged in a long telephone conversation with a cardiologist in Little Rock, one he'd met at a couple of medical conventions.

Alex was able to reassure Bob's family and friends with complete sincerity that Bob would have the best of care and that his chances of a full recovery were very good. With proper follow-up care, there was no reason to believe Bob would not lead a perfectly normal life, he added.

Tears and prayers of gratitude swept through the visitors and well-wishers in response to the optimistic news. A close-knit community, this, Alex reflected, standing to one side of the crowded waiting room as the others embraced and expressed their relief that they hadn't lost their friend.

Alex felt very much the outsider among this group. He watched them somewhat wistfully, thinking that it must be nice to have such a large, devoted support group. He hoped he hadn't given them a false sense of optimism about Bob's future, though he'd tried to be honest.

He'd found it surprisingly difficult to maintain his usual objectivity during Bob's initial evaluation and treatment. He'd made an effort to talk to the young doctor on duty with the clipped professionalism with which he dealt with his colleagues in Boston. And his telephone consultation with the cardiologist in Little Rock had been brisk, impersonal and highly technical. But it had been different this time. Alex couldn't think of Bob as just another set of symptoms, another heart case. Bob was someone he knew and liked. Someone Carly cared about.

His gaze turned automatically to Carly, who was talking quietly to Bob's parents, probably reassuring them that Alex's prognosis was reliable. Carly had said very little to Alex since arriving at the hospital. He tried to believe it was because she'd been so busy answering the dozens of questions that had been thrown at her from Bob's friends. But something told him there was more to it than that.

Carly's expression was shuttered now when she looked at him. Far different from the warmth in her eyes last night. He understood her annoyance with him. She had every right to be irritated that he'd kept something as important as his profession from her, as close as they had become during the past few days. But it was the hurt and disappointment he sensed behind her anger that made him feel like a true heel for deceiving her.

Carly had been deceived once by a man—a doctor—she'd cared about. It bothered Alex greatly that she could even now be comparing him to that shameless fraud she'd known before. He wanted to get her somewhere private. Someplace he could talk to her. Try to make her explain her feelings. Ask her to forgive him.

Alex had never in his life begged a woman's forgiveness. Had never been willing to crawl. With Carly, he knew he would crawl if that's what it took to convince her he had never meant to hurt her.

"Hey, slick." The weary voice behind him made him turn reluctantly away from Carly. Debbie looked exhausted, purple hollows beneath her eyes, her copper hair in wild disarray. She still wore the pale blue nurse's scrubs she'd arrived in earlier, though they'd been neatly pressed then and were deeply wrinkled now.

She spoke again before Alex could say anything. "Maybe I should make that *Dr.* Slick."

He winced at the slight edge in her voice. She wouldn't let him off the hook just because he'd been in the right place at the right time for Bob.

"I guess I should have said something..." he began weakly.

"Gee, ya think?"

Alex sighed in response to her sarcastic comment. "I'm sorry, Debbie. I wasn't deliberately trying to deceive any of you. I just needed a break from being a doctor for a while. Does that make any sense at all to you?"

She thought about it a moment, then shrugged. "Maybe. But I'm not the one you owe an explanation to," she added, looking pointedly across the room toward Carly.

"I know." Alex ran a hand through his hair. "She's pretty mad, isn't she?"

"You could say that," Debbie agreed with apparent satisfaction. "By the way, you looked real suave in those magazine pictures. Like a movie star or something."

"Er...magazine pictures?"

Her eyes still gleaming with relish at his discomfort, she nodded. "You never know what sort of reading material you'll find in a hospital waiting room. Carly found a copy of *Prominence Magazine.* She showed it to me last time you went back to check Bob's stats. You should have told us you were one of the world's most eligible bachelors. We could have arm-wrestled for you or something."

Alex nearly squirmed. He'd been embarrassed enough by the article when it had first come out, and his friends in Boston had teased him so mercilessly. But having Debbie McElroy talk about it was even worse. And he didn't want to think about what Carly's reaction must have been.

"I didn't volunteer for that article," he muttered. "And it really wasn't meant to be taken all that seriously. It was just..."

"No need to explain, Boston," Debbie assured him gravely. "I'm sure your picture has been drooled over by thousands of women who would just love for you to show up on vacation in their part of the country. Of course, Carly might not feel quite the same way. She's never been all that excited about being just another pretty face in a crowd."

Alex's scowl deepened. "You know better than that."

"Did you tell her the truth about who you are?"

"No, but..."

"Then you obviously weren't all that serious about her." Debbie held her pointed chin up defiantly. "I'm very grateful to you for taking care of Bob today, Alex. If you hadn't shown up at his shop when you did...well, I'm grateful. Despite our differences, I'm very fond of Bob, as I guess you know by now, and

I can't bear the thought of losing him. But I'm very fond of Carly, too, and if you hurt her again, you'll have me to answer to. So if you're thinking of her as just another of your conquests, I wish you'd go back to Boston before you risk breaking her heart."

Alex was tempted to tell Debbie to mind her own business. But even as he opened his mouth to do so, he noted again the smudges beneath her eyes and the lines of strain around her mouth. He sighed and fell silent.

Debbie had had a rough day. She'd probably felt powerless to help Bob and was turning her protective instincts toward her other friend instead. How could he blame her for trying to protect Carly from being used and hurt? Carly was fortunate to have a friend who cared so much about her.

"Why don't you get some rest?" he asked, keeping his tone gentle. "You haven't eaten and you look tired. Bob will be transferred within the hour. There's little more you can do for him here."

Debbie nodded and glanced at Bob's family. "I might as well go. He has all the support he needs here."

"He asked me to call you, you know. When we arrived here at the hospital and he was trying not to show how scared he really was, he asked if I would call you. He said he wanted to see you again…just in case."

Debbie's lower lip trembled. "He said something kind of like that to me earlier."

Alex resisted asking her just who was breaking whose heart. He swallowed the words, but Debbie's expression told him that she knew what he was thinking.

She rubbed her eyes with her fingertips, the gesture weary and dispirited. "I need to go home...to think about some things. Will you tell Carly I'll see her tomorrow?"

"I'll tell her."

Impulsively, Debbie rose to brush a quick kiss against Alex's cheek, taking him by surprise—and maybe herself, as well. "Thank you for saving his life," she murmured.

"Get some rest, Debbie," Alex muttered, both touched and embarrassed by her gesture. She nodded, turned and hurried away.

Alex glanced across the room to find Carly watching him with little expression on her face. He wondered what she was thinking. He wondered how soon he could get her alone to ask her.

Carly took the coward's way out. She slipped out of the hospital among a group of Bob's other friends, giving Alex little opportunity to detain her. She knew he made an effort to catch up with her, but she was able to get into her car and escape before he could do more than call her name—which she pretended not to hear.

She hated herself for acting this way, like a sulking teenager, but she couldn't face him tonight. She was too tired, too drained, her emotions still too raw. The photographs in that magazine were still too clear in her mind.

The photos had shown Alex in a glittering, wealthy world that Carly had only seen on television and movie screens. The women at his side were beautiful, sophisticated, worldly-looking. The article had identified them as lawyers and businesswomen and even a fairly well-known television actress. A couple of them had been doctors, specialists of one sort or another, but Carly doubted she would have much in common with them, either. There hadn't been a simple country doctor in the bunch.

What had made Carly even consider that maybe Alex might like her home so much that he would be tempted to remain? Had she really been foolish enough to indulge in that improbable fantasy, just because he had made love to her so beautifully?

Betty was waiting impatiently when Carly got home. She demanded news of Bob's condition almost before Carly could close the door behind her.

Studying Carly's face closely, Betty lifted a hand to her chest. "Bob isn't doing well, is he? Oh, Carly..."

"Bob is doing very well, considering what he's been through today," Carly said quickly, reaching out to take her grandmother's hands. "There's no reason to believe at this point that he won't recover completely after his surgery."

"Oh, thank God." Betty blinked back tears. "You looked so grim when you came in that I was afraid the news was very bad."

Carly shook her head and tried to smile. "Sorry, Granny. I'm just tired."

"Of course you are. Have you had anything to eat?"

Carly tried to remember. "Not since lunch," she said. "I'll make a sandwich."

"You'll do no such thing. Go wash up and change into something comfortable and I'll make you something to eat."

It must have been because she was so tired that

Carly felt like crying as she headed up the stairs. The stress of worrying about Bob. The long hours of waiting, watching for changes in his condition, making sure he was stabilized enough for the transfer. The people who'd surrounded her, begging her to assure them their friend would recover. Her grandmother's loving solicitude.

All reason enough to bring tears to her eyes.

She surely wasn't on the verge of tears because Alex Keating had turned out to be someone other than she'd thought. Despite all the silly proclamations she'd made to herself in the afterglow of fabulous lovemaking, she hadn't really fallen in love with him. Hadn't really expected a lifelong promise from this man who was only passing through.

Finding out the truth about him and about the life he led only reinforced her assurance that there could be nothing lasting between them. She thought of a photograph taken of him at a high-society charity affair in Boston last year, and she winced at how he must have perceived the down-home fund-raiser at the Seventy-Six Community Center, which had been followed by the confrontation with the local rednecks.

The odds of Alex Keating remaining here—or even visiting again anytime soon—were slim, indeed.

If it hurt this much just to think about him leaving, how would she feel when it actually happened? When the time came that she had to say goodbye? Would it be any easier if she said it now, before she spent any more time with him and risked falling even harder? Or did she want to spend as much free time with him as possible during the days they had left, storing up memories to savor for the rest of her life?

Emotionally battered and confused, she pasted on

a placid expression for her grandmother's sake and went down to the kitchen.

A light supper of cold chicken, pasta salad and a crusty wheat roll was waiting for her on the table. "This looks wonderful," she said, gratefully picking up her fork. "I hadn't realized how hungry I was until now."

Her grandmother set a glass of juice beside Carly's plate. "You could have knocked me over with a feather when you told me on the phone that Alex was overseeing Bob's care. I wonder why he didn't mention that he's a cardiologist?"

Carly swallowed past a sudden constriction in her throat. "I really don't know."

"You're annoyed with him," Betty murmured, studying Carly perceptively.

"A little."

"I'm sure he had a good reason for not telling us."

"You always think the best of people you like." It wasn't a criticism, merely a statement of fact.

"He's a good man, Carly. Give him a chance to explain."

Carly nodded. "I'll listen to his explanation. But he doesn't really owe us one. To be quite honest, it's none of our business what Alex does or doesn't do in Boston."

Betty frowned. "I'm not sure what you mean."

"It's not as if we even know him all that well. We're merely people he met on his vacation. I doubt that we'll ever see him again after he leaves in a few days."

"I don't believe that, Carly. And I don't think you do, either."

Carly looked at her plate. "There's no reason to

believe otherwise. Alex doesn't belong here. This isn't his world."

"He's grown very fond of you. Anyone can see that. I think he'll want to see you again."

"I'm not interested in being his girl in this particular port," Carly answered coolly. "Long-distance relationships simply don't last. And I've never been interested in starting something that's destined to end badly."

"Carly..."

Carly shook her head and pushed her plate away, the food only half-eaten. "Please, Granny. I'm really very tired. It's been a long, stressful day. I'm just not up to dealing with your matchmaking right now."

"All right," Betty said, turning her face away. "We won't talk about it anymore tonight."

Carly sighed and cursed herself for hurting the one person who mattered most to her in the world. "I'm sorry. I didn't mean to snap at you. Please forgive me."

Betty gave her a tender little smile. "You're tired. You don't want to talk about serious things just now. Finish your dinner and then go up to bed."

"I'm full. I just need some sleep."

"Of course. Go on up. I'll put these things away and then I'm turning in, as well."

Carly nodded. "Sleep in tomorrow. I'll grab a bagel for breakfast and slip out quietly. I'll call you later in the morning to let you know how Bob's doing."

"I'd appreciate that. You're sure he'll be okay?"

"He should be," Carly answered with a touch of irony. "He's had one of the best cardiologists in the world taking care of him."

* * *

Alex got very little sleep that night. He spent much of the time pacing, cursing himself for not telling Carly everything about himself that first night he dined with her and her grandmother, for becoming involved with these people, who'd been getting along quite nicely before he'd quite literally stumbled into their lives, for hurting a woman who deserved it less than anyone he'd ever met.

Would she forgive him? And if she accepted his apology, then what? What was he hoping would happen between them in the long term?

He'd never felt this way about another woman. Whether it was love or simply a desire more intense than he'd even imagined before, he didn't expect it to go away soon.

Boston had begun to seem empty and lonely to him during the past few years, his work the only thing that truly mattered to him. Now that he'd met Carly, would his work be enough?

The town was abuzz with gossip the next day, much of which Carly heard during her rounds at the hospital and from her patients at the clinic. Debbie muttered that the staff at the hospital were carrying on as if Harrison Ford or some other major Hollywood star had dropped in for a casual visit. Half the nurses had fallen in love with Alex, she said with a moue of disgust. The other half had been terrified of him.

Word had gotten out about the magazine article, and that only added to the mystique of the good-looking man who'd come into their area on a solitary vacation and made such an impression. Giving Ronnie Mayo a long-deserved setdown. Saving Bob's life.

Spending so much time with Carly—something else the gossips seemed inclined to speculate about.

It was a long day.

Word from Little Rock was that Bob had come through surgery very well and would recuperate in CCU there for several days before being sent home. Carly sent word that she would take care of Francis for him and told him to feel free to contact her if he needed anything else.

Debbie wasn't particularly talkative that day, and Carly didn't push her. She could tell that her friend was trying to deal with the emotions she'd been forced to face when Bob's life had hung in the balance. Carly knew exactly how it felt to be torn by love and fear. And she sympathized with her friend.

It was nearly 6:00 p.m. by the time Carly was able to drive home. She hadn't heard from Alex all day. She wondered if he was giving her time to get over her irritation with him or if he was waiting for her to contact him for an explanation of his silence.

She was half-tempted to drive to his cabin and demand that explanation. But cowardice made her drive home, instead. When she saw Alex's car in the driveway, she knew the time for stalling was at an end. Ready or not, she had to face him.

As she had expected, Carly found her grandmother hovering solicitously over Alex, who sat on the sofa, a cup of tea in his hand, a plate of home-baked cookies on the table in front of him. He set down the tea when Carly entered and rose to greet her.

"Hello, Carly."

"Alex." Carly nodded at him, then kissed her grandmother's cheek. "Hi, Granny."

"Hello, sweetheart. How was your day?"

"Busy, as usual. Ryan Kirkpatrick broke his arm again."

Betty clucked and shook her head. "That boy. He's not going to have an unbroken bone in his body if he doesn't start being more careful."

"That's what I told him. All he wanted to know was what color cast he could have this time."

Alex frowned. "How old is this boy?"

Wondering why he'd asked, Carly answered, "He's thirteen."

"Have you considered child abuse? Repeated injuries are often a sign of violence in the home."

Carly answered coolly, feeling as if he'd challenged her medical skills. "Roy and Patty Kirkpatrick are not child abusers. They're rodeo enthusiasts. Ryan gets injured because he's in junior bull-riding competitions. It's not something I would want my own son to do, if I had one, but it's his choice and his parents support him in it. That isn't against the law."

"Roy was a national rodeo star a few years back, before he settled down to raise his family," Betty added. "Their daughter, Angela, is an accomplished barrel racer. Fortunately, she isn't as reckless and injury-prone as her younger brother."

Alex nodded. "I don't hear about a lot of rodeo injuries in Boston," he admitted. "Guess I just leaped to the wrong conclusion."

"We have our share of child abuse and neglect around here," Carly said, wrinkling her nose in distaste. "I know what to watch for, and I always report it when I suspect it."

"I wasn't questioning your competence," Alex said quietly. "I was merely trying to contribute to the conversation."

"Of course you were, dear. Carly knows that." Betty patted his arm, then glanced at the clock on the mantel. "If you two will excuse me, I need to go freshen up. Jennilee Hardcastle is picking me up for prayer meeting in half an hour, and afterward we're going to Bennie Bradley's house for coffee and cake. I'm sure you two have plenty to talk about."

Carly bit her lower lip. She'd rather hoped her grandmother would stay as a buffer between her and Alex. She had never realized what a coward she was.

Carly and Alex made polite conversation about Bob's condition while Betty was upstairs. Again, Alex seemed so natural in doctor mode that Carly couldn't believe she hadn't suspected the truth.

Betty left in a whirl of instructions and farewells, and the house seemed very quiet after the door closed behind her. Carly shoved her hands in her pockets, trying to think of something to say.

"Should we call the hospital in Little Rock and check on Bob?" she asked, before launching into that so-important conversation she knew was inevitable that evening.

Alex looked at his watch. "I thought I'd call in about an hour, after the new shift takes over and checks his stats."

"The news sounded good today, didn't it?" she asked, needing the professional reassurance one more time.

Alex answered patiently, "Everything looks very promising."

She made a face and ran a hand through her hair. "I guess I just need to be reminded every so often. When I thought that we might lose Bob..." She shuddered.

Alex nodded grimly. "I like him, too. I was terrified that he would go into full arrest on the way to the hospital yesterday. To be honest, I'm not used to getting that rattled by a medical emergency."

Carly glanced at him skeptically. "I thought sheer terror was a part of this profession. I'm always a wreck when I think I'm going to lose a patient, though I do my best not to let it show. At least, not until later, when I'm alone."

"I don't know most of my patients as well as you do," he confessed. "I'm the specialist who's called in by their regular doctors. I see them, treat them, operate on some of them, then send them back to their primary care physicians for follow-up care. Sometimes I see them a couple more times, but I don't get to know them or their families very well."

"That's one reason I wasn't interested in specializing. I like getting to know my patients on a personal basis."

"Even when it breaks your heart to lose one?"

She swallowed hard and nodded. "Even then."

Alex reached out to touch her cheek. "Your patients are very lucky to have you."

She wanted to cover his hand with hers, to burrow into his shoulder and try to release the tension that had been building in her since she'd gotten the call about Bob and learned the truth about Alex. She forced herself to keep her distance.

Her voice was deliberately cool when she said, "I think it's time for us to talk about your reasons for not telling me sooner that you're a doctor. Was it because you didn't think it was any of my business what you do for a living?"

Twelve

Alex winced in response to Carly's bluntly stated question. "You have every right to ask what I do for a living, Carly. After what happened between us, you should feel free to ask anything you want about me."

Looking down at her tightly entwined hands, she lifted one shoulder in a slight shrug. "We went to bed together one time. That doesn't necessarily give me any rights where you're concerned—or vice versa."

Alex scowled. He reached out to cover her hands with his own, his grip firm, her skin cool to his touch. "Don't make it sound as though we shared nothing more than casual, convenient sex. It was more than that, damn it, and you know it."

She didn't pursue that subject but returned to her original question. "Why didn't you tell me?"

He wished he had an answer for her. Or for himself.

"I don't know," he admitted. "It just...never seemed like the right time to bring it up."

She looked at him in open disbelief. Knowing she deserved more than that, he struggled to come up with a better explanation.

"I think I mentioned that this is the first vacation I've taken in a very long time."

She nodded.

He turned his hands palms up on his knees, a gesture of stress and weariness. "I'd reached a point where every beep of my pager, every shout of my name were enough to set my teeth on edge. I'd gotten surly and irritable and demanding, and my co-workers were beginning to suffer from it. When I started worrying about my patients suffering from my burnout, I knew it was time to get away for a while."

"I can understand that. I haven't had a vacation in quite a while myself. I've been thinking of trying to take some time off next summer. But—"

"But that still doesn't explain why I didn't say anything to you," he broke in, knowing what she was going to say.

She nodded again.

"When I was first brought in to you, I could hardly say anything coherent," he reminded her, wincing at the ignominious memory. "For that evening, I was your patient, and my profession didn't matter."

"And the next day?"

He shrugged. "By then, I was enjoying the novelty of being treated like a regular joe. For a change, people were listing their medical symptoms for someone else at parties, and no one wanted to get me involved in endless discussions of managed health care, or new developments in cardiac surgery, or whether the FDA is too cautious in approving new meds, or any of the other tired and boring discussions that take place at my social events in Boston. And no one was giving me a hard time about that stupid article, because few people around here had read it. I just..."

He groped for a summation, then raised one hand. "I was having a good time. And it had been so long since I'd been able to relax that I wanted to hold on to it for a while."

"And you were going to tell me the truth Monday night, just before I was called to deliver Nancy's baby."

"Yes."

She eyed him considerably, and no matter how hard he tried, he was unable to fathom her expression.

"Were you also going to tell me that you're one of the world's most eligible bachelors?"

Alex felt his cheeks warm in response to her dry question. "That article was *not* my idea. I was approached by someone on the magazine staff, and I was under the impression that the article was about how difficult it is for a very busy doctor to sustain a relationship."

Carly nodded as if she understood that sentiment, at least. "It was a nice article," she conceded. "Very flattering to you."

"My friend Tony said it made me sound like Saint Alex of Boston," he muttered. "If I'd had any idea how much attention the stupid thing would get..."

Carly suddenly smiled. "Have you had a few volunteers to help you out of your lonely state?"

"A few?" Alex rolled his eyes. "You wouldn't believe it. Letters, phone calls to the hospital. Flower deliveries, for crying out loud. One woman even wrote me that she wouldn't expect any of my time or attention as long as her name was added to my checking account and credit cards."

Carly snickered. "And she thought that offer would appeal to you because...?"

"Heaven only knows."

Carly ran a hand through her layered hair, leaving

it appealingly tousled. "Thank you for explaining, Alex. I suppose I understand now why you were reluctant to tell everyone around here who you are."

"I wasn't sure how you would react," he confessed. "Knowing that we shared a profession could have given us even more in common, or it might have made you more aware of the differences between us."

"Because you work with state-of-the-art medical labs and equipment, while I make do with what must seem to be extremely primitive conditions?" She wrinkled her nose. "Don't think that hasn't occurred to me."

"I didn't want you to feel defensive for any reason."

She squirmed a little on the couch beside him. "The way I did earlier, when I snapped at you for asking if I'd considered child abuse in Ryan's family."

He nodded. "Exactly. I really wasn't trying to imply that I'm a more experienced or competent physician. Child abuse is obviously not something I deal with in cardiac practice. It was just a question that crossed my mind when I heard you mention that a child had had several broken bones."

"I'm sorry I overreacted."

"And I'm sorry I hurt you by not being honest with you from the beginning."

"You didn't..." She fell silent.

"I hurt you," he corrected, knowing what she'd been about to say and why she hadn't been able to complete the lie.

Carly sighed and moistened her lips. "Maybe a little."

"That's the one thing I never wanted to do." He

reached out to cup her face in his hands. "Not to you, of all people."

She lifted her hands to cover his. "Alex..."

He lowered his head, kissing her for the first time since they'd parted at the hospital after making love. Her taste was familiar now, her mouth no mystery to him. But this kiss was no less exciting to him than the first.

He lingered. Savored. Nipped at her lower lip, then soothed the invisible bite marks with the tip of his tongue. Only then did he allow himself to deepen the embrace, sliding past the serrated edges of her straight white teeth to lose himself in her.

Carly made a little sound deep in her throat, a murmur of resignation, of pleasure, of need. He recognized the sentiments, because he experienced them all himself. He'd tried to tell himself that all he felt for Carly was desire. Infatuation. Fascination.

But there was more. So very much more. For the first time in his forty years, Robert Alexander Keating had fallen in love.

The truth flashed through his mind with vivid clarity, refusing to be denied. It brought with it a tangle of emotions that included joy, fear, hope and trepidation. He was afraid that a relationship between them could not possibly work out—and equally certain that he had no choice but to try.

He couldn't imagine just walking away from love when it had taken him so long to find it.

He drew back only an inch, his eyes locked with Carly's. Her lids were heavy, her eyes bright beneath them, her cheeks flushed, her mouth glistening from his kiss. And he wanted her so badly he ached with it.

"How long will your grandmother be gone?"

Carly cleared her throat. "A couple of hours."

He kissed the end of her nose, the soft curve of her right cheek. "Want to go out for something to eat?"

Her lower lip trembled. Her hands clenched his shoulders convulsively. "We...um...we could find something to eat here."

He nibbled her earlobe, toying with the small diamond stud she wore there, touching his tongue to the scented hollow behind her ear. "That would be fine with me."

"Mmm?" Her voice had grown thick, distracted. "What would?"

"Finding something here," he murmured, smiling against the skin of her throat, which she had obligingly arched to grant him better access.

Carly slid her hand down the front of his shirt, resting it over his pounding heart. "Where?"

"Here," he muttered, covering her mouth with his again.

She wrapped her arms around his neck and pulled him closer. They fell back against the couch, Alex's weight pressing Carly into the deep cushions. He swept his hands restlessly over her body, reacquainting himself with the slender curves he'd memorized the last time they'd been alone together. Already he knew her body so well, knew what made her shiver, where to touch to make her moan deep in her chest.

She moaned now.

"Alex?" Her voice was ragged.

"Mmm?"

"Have I..." She paused to kiss him again, then continued, "Have I ever shown you my bedroom?"

"No. I don't believe you have."

She caught his head between her hands and kissed him until his ears buzzed. "Would you like to see it now?" she asked, when she finally released his mouth.

He wasn't at all sure that he could walk up the stairs with any dignity. His knees didn't feel exactly rock-steady. But he found himself willing to risk it.

"Yes," he growled, pushing himself upright. "I would like to see your room now."

Carly stood and held out her hand to him, making no effort to hide her trembling. Alex's hand was not quite steady, either, when he reached out to link his fingers with hers.

"Carly?"

Alex's deep voice roused Carly from her warm, contented drifting. Without opening her eyes, she asked, "Hmm?"

"Your grandmother will be home soon. Shouldn't we get dressed?"

She sighed and snuggled more deeply into his shoulder. "Mmm-hmm."

"I'm not sure she would appreciate finding us this way. She'd probably go looking for her shotgun."

"Granny doesn't have a shotgun," Carly murmured, her eyes still closed. "She's got a twenty-two."

"Oh, that's encouraging."

Carly smiled against his damp skin. "It belonged to my grandfather. I don't think Granny knows how to use it."

"Bet she swings a mean frying pan, though."

Carly chuckled and finally, reluctantly opened her eyes. "That she does."

Smiling, Alex lifted a hand to the rapidly fading bruise at his temple—the injury that had brought him to Carly in the first place. "Since I'm really not up to another head injury so soon, I think I'll opt for discretion. Let's get dressed."

Carly exhaled gustily. "If you insist."

Unexpectedly, Alex pulled her up to press a hard, heated kiss against her mouth, which was still slightly tender from all the kisses that had come before. "Sometime," he said, his voice gruff, "we're going to have the entire night together. We're going to make love all night, and then wake in each other's arms and make love until night falls again."

Carly groaned and tilted her head down to kiss him again. "Keep talking like that and I'll never let you out of this bed."

His smile was crooked. "Keep kissing me like that and I'll never want to leave."

Their words hung in the air for a moment, filled with meaning neither wanted to examine very closely just then.

Carly suddenly dropped her gaze, unable to meet Alex's eyes, unable to think about his leaving. About how little chance there would be for them to spend an entire night together, much less a night followed by an entire day.

Alex would be leaving in only a few more days, she reminded herself as she pulled on her clothes. He had a life to get back to in Boston. An important career. People who depended on him. Who needed him. Carly couldn't think now about how much *she* needed him.

It was while he was having breakfast in a local diner the next morning that Alex became aware he was being regarded with a measure of awe by the locals, even the ones he'd met and who had treated him with casual warmth before. Obviously, the grapevine had been busy about who he was and what he had done.

He was no longer just Alex, a not-very-skillful fisherman who happened to be handy with his fists when harassed by a couple of bullies. Now he was Dr. Robert Alexander Keating, the man who'd saved the life of a local citizen and who had been featured in an article in a national magazine.

He was a hero, a celebrity.

He'd preferred being just Alex.

"Dr. Keating."

Alex turned his head to find a florid-faced, paunchy, fifty-something doctor approaching his table. Alex had met the doctor at the hospital but couldn't recall his name. Griffin? Gibson? Gresham, he remembered.

"Good morning, Doctor," he said with a polite nod.

"Have you heard about Bob Calhoun?" Gresham spoke in a jovial, broad country accent. "I've been told he's making a steady recovery."

"Yes, he's doing remarkably well."

"He was damned lucky to have one of the country's top specialists here for his initial care." Gresham punched Alex genially in the arm. "Most folks around here have to settle for me or Carly or the couple other general practitioners who work in this area. We get a lot of heart complications due to smoking and poor eating habits and the aging of our population, but we usually have to send them elsewhere for specialized care.''

''I'm sure you and Carly are both excellent primary care physicians,'' Alex replied, feeling as if it were expected of him.

Gresham shrugged modestly. ''My patients seem satisfied,'' he admitted. ''And Carly's darned good. I've got to admit, I was a little worried when I heard a young woman practically right out of school was buying the clinic, but she proved herself quick enough around here. There's one sharp brain in that pretty head of hers.''

Alex wondered if Gresham talked this way around Carly. He couldn't imagine that she would either appreciate or tolerate such condescension.

''Say, Alex,'' Gresham continued, suddenly talking like Alex's new best friend, ''what do you say we have lunch together later today? You can tell me what it's like to work in one of those big-time, big-money medical clinics and I can clue you in on how we have to get by with Band-Aids and rubbing alcohol.''

''I'm sorry, but I already have lunch plans for today,'' Alex lied with just the right touch of regret.

''Some other time?''

Alex murmured something noncommittal.

Gresham sighed gustily when the pager on his belt began to beep. ''Duty calls. See you later, Al.''

Alex really hated being called ''Al.'' His smile felt stiff when he watched Gresham hurry away. There was only one doctor Alex wanted to spend time with that day.

Carly was in an examining room with Gus Eberle when she was informed that Dr. Keating was waiting to see her when she had a spare minute. She started to nod and send word that she would be with him as quickly as possible, and then she hesitated, glancing thoughtfully at her patient.

"Gus, would you mind if I have a colleague of mine come in and take a look at you?" she asked politely. "He's a heart specialist, and I'd like to have a consultation with him about your treatment."

Gus's eyebrows, which had been lowered in concern because Carly had been telling him that his blood pressure was no lower than it had been the last time she'd seen him, rose in sudden interest. "Is that the doctor that beat up Ronnie Mayo and saved Reverend Calhoun's life?"

Carly nodded, amused by Alex's contrasting claims to fame. "Dr. Alex Keating from Boston. You met him when he was having lunch with Debbie, remember?"

"Yeah. 'Course, I didn't know he was a doctor then."

Neither had Carly or Debbie at the time, but she chose not to mention that now. "Would you like me to ask him in?"

"Sure. Maybe he'll know of some fancy new medicine I can take," Gus said hopefully.

"Could be," Carly agreed, though as long as Gus continued his current diet, kept smoking and regularly neglected to take his blood pressure medication, Carly didn't think Alex could make any great progress. He was a doctor, not a miracle worker.

Carly met Alex in the hallway outside the examining room. "You really don't mind taking a look at him?" she asked, after explaining the situation to him.

Alex was already looking through Gus's file. "Not at all. I remember meeting him at the steak house. Seemed like a nice guy."

"He is," Carly admitted, her throat tight. "I like him very much. But I'm going to lose him if I can't convince him to take better care of himself. I've tried to get him to a specialist in Little Rock, but he refuses to go. I'm the only doctor he'll see."

Alex touched her shoulder, the gesture meant to comfort. "I should be flattered, I suppose," he said with a slight smile.

She would have liked to hug him. Aware of their surroundings, she answered lightly instead, "Well, you did beat up Ronnie Mayo. That makes you okay in Gus's book."

Alex rolled his eyes. "Am I ever going to live that down around here?"

Since Carly didn't think he would be staying long enough to worry about it, she didn't answer.

Gus greeted Alex warmly, swapping small talk with him while Alex listened to his heart, palpated his neck, checked the circulation in his limbs and interjected an occasional question.

"You've had an eventful vacation, haven't you, Doc?" Gus asked as Alex finally stepped back, making a few notes on Gus's chart with Carly's permission.

Alex nodded. "Except for Bob's health scare, I've had a very nice time."

"Think you'll be back to visit us again?"

Carly almost held her breath as she waited for Alex's answer. That was a question she had wanted to ask herself.

"I'm quite sure I'll be back," Alex answered easily. "It's a beautiful area, with some of the nicest people I've ever met. You're one of them, by the way. Too bad you won't be here next time I visit."

Gus's eyes rounded. "What do you mean?"

Alex shrugged and tapped Gus's chart. "You're fifty-nine, right? I'd be surprised if you see sixty."

Gus's color faded along with his smile.

Carly bit her lip, wondering if she'd made a mistake calling in Alex. She'd known that he wasn't one to get personally involved with his patients, but she hadn't expected him to be quite this detached.

"It's that bad, Doc?" Gus looked at both Alex and Carly as he spoke.

"It is unless something changes drastically in the next few weeks—or days," Alex answered with another faint shrug. "I'm sorry, Gus, but no doctor can force you to take care of your health. That's something you have to help us with. I can't see from these charts that you've tried to help Dr. Fletcher at all."

"I've cut back on my smoking," Gus said, turning argumentative now. "I used to smoke three packs a day, and I'm down to a pack, a pack and a half now."

Alex shook his head. "Not good enough. You've got to quit. I'd advise cold turkey. There are prescription medications that can help you through it, as well as some other aids you can try. But the cigarettes are killing you. So is your weight, by the way. Your heart simply can't take the strain you're putting on it. You got any grandkids, Gus?"

"Got a couple of grandsons," Gus answered in a sullen mutter. "Five and seven. Good boys."

"I'm sure they are. Bet they're crazy about their grandpa, too."

"They think he walks on water," Carly said

quickly, smiling at Gus with an attempt at reassurance. "Everyone knows how close Gus and his grandsons are."

"Ever take them fishing?" Alex asked.

Gus nodded, his expression lighting a little. "Yeah. Their father works in a bank. Doesn't like to get his hands dirty with bait and fish. Someone's got to teach those boys to fish."

"Who's going to teach them if you aren't around?" Alex asked simply.

Gus winced. "I, uh..."

"Dr. Fletcher told me there's a specialist in Little Rock she's been wanting you to see. I think that sounds like a good idea. There are several procedures available to greatly increase your chance of being around awhile longer for those boys—as long as you cooperate with the specialist's instructions, of course."

"Yeah, Doc Fletcher's mentioned that she wanted me to see someone else. I guess I just didn't want to admit how bad off I was. Thought I could handle it on my own."

"Will you let her set you up an appointment?"

Gus looked at Carly with an apologetic expression. "Sure. You set it up, I'll go, Doc."

Carly gave him a bright smile. "You've made the right decision, Gus. I'll have Debbie call and set up an appointment for as soon as we can get you in. I'll let you know when it will be. Your daughter will probably want to go with you. She's been worried about you, you know."

"I know. Seems like everyone's been worried but me."

Alex closed Gus's file. "So, how would you like

to give me some fishing pointers next time I'm in the area, Gus?''

The older man gave a semblance of his usual broad grin. ''I'll be here, Doc.''

''Glad to hear that.''

Carly escorted Alex into her office after they'd taken their departure from Gus. She closed the door and turned to study him with her hands on her hips.

He cleared his throat. ''I didn't step on your professional toes, did I? You *did* ask me to talk to him.''

''I never let my ego get in the way of my patients' welfare,'' she informed him. ''If it takes another doctor's opinion to convince them to follow instructions, then I'm all for it.''

''No ego? Don't let that get out. Our profession has a reputation to maintain.''

She shook her head. ''I have to admit, your bedside manner startled me.''

He pushed his hands into his pockets. ''Sometimes you've got to get their attention before they'll listen.''

''You're a fraud, Robert Alexander Keating.''

He lifted an eyebrow, obviously not certain what she meant. ''I beg your pardon?''

''You implied to me that you don't get personally involved with your patients. That they're nothing more than lists of symptoms to you. And I say that's bull.''

He looked skeptical. ''And you've come to this conclusion on what basis?''

''The way you asked Gus about his grandchildren. The way you zeroed in on the one argument he couldn't brush off. That strategy came from experience, Keating, not just circumstance.''

''I can generally tell something about my patients

from talking to them,'' he admitted. ''That's part of being a good doctor. But as far as remembering them after they leave my office, well...that's when they often become nothing more than statistics in my files. I've become increasingly aware of that as I've watched you interact with your patients...your friends. You have a connection with them that goes beyond their medical charts. And I admire you tremendously for it.''

Acting on sheer impulse, Carly took a step toward him, cupped his face between her hands and planted a firm kiss on his mouth.

''What was that for?'' he asked, though he obviously wasn't complaining.

''I admire you tremendously, too,'' she replied, her heart filled with emotion.

Alex put his hands on her hips and started to draw her closer, but Carly forced herself to be practical and slipped away from him. ''I have patients waiting. Would you...?'' She hesitated, suddenly awkward.

''Would I what?''

''I was going to suggest that you hang around and observe, if you're interested in the daily operation of a rural primary care clinic. But that's probably not the way you'd like to spend a day of your vacation, so if—''

''I would love to,'' he cut in quickly.

''Are you sure? It's a pretty day to be outside.''

He shrugged. ''I'd rather be with you.''

The little thrill that went through her in response to those words made her feel almost like slapping herself. *Snap out of it, Carly. Stop acting like a lovesick teenager.*

She straightened her shoulders, smoothed her white

coat and nodded with a pretense of professionalism. "I can't promise excitement, Dr. Keating, but I can guarantee variety. Starting with the two-week-old baby in examining room three who's here for his well-baby checkup."

"The only babies I've seen lately have had congenital heart defects," Alex replied. "Seeing a well baby will be a nice change. Lead on, Dr. Fletcher."

Thirteen

Alex spent the rest of Thursday and Friday as close to Carly as he could be without interfering in her work. He observed her with several of her patients and had lunch with her when she had a few minutes to grab a bite. When she was busy with paperwork, he entertained himself by fishing, watching nature, sight-seeing—and counting the minutes until he saw Carly again.

During those sight-seeing excursions, he looked more closely at the area than he had before. He saw the wrenching poverty—the decrepit mobile homes and shacklike structures some called home, the mud yards filled with old vehicles that hadn't run in years, the clotheslines holding sadly tattered garments, the dogs and chickens scratching in rocky dirt.

Alex thought of the neighborhoods in which he had grown up and practiced his vocation, and realized that these people lived very hard lives. The rural isolation contributed to their problems, since public transportation was practically nonexistent, and the scattered homes were well beyond walking distance of grocery stores, medical facilities, libraries, even public assistance agencies.

He found more affluent areas, of course. New housing developments and a few new retail establishments, small signs that developing industry in the area was slowly beginning to make a difference. But there was still a long way to go. And Carly was doing all she could to make her neighbors' lives easier.

On Thursday evening Alex dined with Carly and her grandmother at their house, after which he discreetly returned to his cabin—though not without first giving Carly a good-night kiss that left them both panting and aroused.

He was becoming more aware with each passing minute that his vacation was drawing to a close. He was to fly back to Boston on Tuesday, leaving him only four full days to spend with Carly. He didn't even want to think about that until he absolutely had to.

He had asked her to meet him at his cabin when she left her clinic after working late again on Friday evening.

Alex had a surprise waiting when Carly arrived.

"You've cooked dinner?" She seemed both stunned and delighted when she saw what he had done. "I assumed we would eat out. This is so much nicer. What a lovely surprise."

He'd set the small round oak table with the vinyl place mats, sturdy pottery dishes and unadorned flatware provided for renters of the rustic cabin. He'd purchased wineglasses, candles and flowers in town when he bought supplies for the meal, and had used them to add a touch of elegance to the simple place settings. A bottle of wine cooled in a bucket of ice, more purchases from his hasty shopping trip.

"I cooked," he agreed, holding her chair for her. "Are you surprised that I did or that I can?"

"Both," she admitted with a smile. "Alex, this looks wonderful."

He set a fresh garden salad in front of her, another at his own place. And then he took his seat, picked up his fork and smiled at her, pleased with her reaction to his efforts. "I wanted you all to myself tonight."

"I want that, too," she said, smiling at him in a way that made him wonder if he'd be able to swallow a bite.

He reached hastily for the wine, pouring a generous portion into both their glasses.

Carly seemed to thoroughly enjoy the meal. She ate every bite of her salad, then raved about the entrée that followed, fresh trout stuffed with wild rice, and crisp steamed asparagus on the side.

"Did you catch these fish?"

He grinned. "Yes. I brought the recipe with me from Boston—just in case I had any luck."

"This is wonderful," she almost purred, her eyes closing as she swallowed a bite of the flaky fish. "Do I taste lemon?"

"I added some lemon zest to the rice. Do you like it?"

"Mmm. No wonder thousands of women want to marry you."

He cleared his throat. "Maybe not thousands," he muttered, slightly embarrassed by the reference to the magazine article.

"Who taught you to cook? Your mother?"

He snorted. "The only thing I remember my mother ever cooking was coffee. And she makes that badly."

Carly chuckled. "Then who did the cooking at your house? Your dad?"

"Our cooks," he corrected her. "A woman named

Lucille for the first twelve years of my life. After she retired, there were others. I liked hanging out in the kitchen. My parents were gone a lot, and I got lonely sometimes. The cooks always took the time to talk to me, let me lick the spoon, experiment with recipes. I liked it."

Carly reached across the table to cover his hand with hers. "You didn't have a very happy childhood, did you?"

He shrugged. "I wasn't particularly unhappy. I had nothing to compare it to. My parents love me in their own way. We had plenty of money. I had the intelligence, encouragement and opportunity to become whatever I wanted. And we always had really nice cooks."

Carly drew back her hand and shook her head, her expression suddenly pensive. "We come from such different worlds, Alex. It's a wonder we even speak the same language. Though sometimes I wonder about that when that east coast accent of yours takes over."

He smiled faintly in acknowledgement of the weak joke. "You make it sound as though we have nothing in common."

She lifted an eyebrow, as if she found that statement perfectly reasonable.

"What was your major in college?" he demanded.

"Biology."

"So was mine."

She wasn't impressed. "Lots of premed students major in biology."

"Remember the MCAT?"

She shuddered. "As if I could forget the nine-hour

exam that determined whether or not I would get into medical school.''

''It was hell, wasn't it? Months of cramming. No sleep. Headaches. Nervous stomach cramps.''

Carly grimaced. ''I went through all of that. I was so scared. I just knew I would get in that room and forget everything I'd learned in three years of undergraduate work, that my score would be so low, no medical school would accept me.''

''I was the same way. I thought I would be doomed to go to work for my father if I didn't do exceptionally well on that exam.''

''Every aspiring medical student sweats the MCAT,'' Carly said.

Alex wasn't giving up. ''Remember medical school? How lost you felt the first few weeks? How long that second year felt? How tired you got working graveyard shift as an intern? Remember how it felt to lose your first patient?''

Her face went stark. ''I remember.''

This time it was Alex who reached across the table. ''So do I. We have as much in common as we have in contrast, Carly. Don't write us off without giving us a chance.''

''A chance for what, Alex? You'll only be here a few more days.''

His fingers tightened convulsively on hers. ''Then let's not waste them,'' he said.

She set down her fork and pushed away her nearly empty plate. ''You're right. I think it's time for dessert, don't you?''

''Definitely.'' He stood, pulled her to her feet and swept her impulsively into his arms. ''We'll have the cake I bought later.''

"I think it's going to be much later," Carly murmured, locking her arms around his neck.

They had their cake sometime around midnight. Sharing one plate on the bed between them, they sat cross-legged on the rumpled comforter, holding forks in one hand and wineglasses in the other. Carly wore nothing but one of Alex's shirts; Alex wore sweatpants. The only light in the room came from the low-wattage bulb in the lamp beside the bed. Her pager lay on the nightstand, but it was mercifully quiet. She could hardly remember a time when she'd been more content.

Alex met her gaze over the rim of his glass, his smile crinkling the corners of his eyes. "You look quite decadent," he murmured.

She smiled, picturing herself as he must see her, her hair rumpled, his shirt unbuttoned to the tops of her breasts, her unpainted lips glistening from the wine she'd just sipped, her bare legs tucked beneath her. She rather liked being decadent for a change. As long as it was with Alex, of course.

"And you look..." She studied him a moment before completing the sentence. His dark hair tumbled over his forehead. His blue eyes glittered from within shadows cast across his face by the dim bedside lamp. His broad, bare shoulders rippled with his movements when he lifted his wineglass lazily to his mouth. "Dangerous."

His eyebrows rose. "In what way?"

In every way, she could have answered. But the greatest danger he posed was to her heart. He'd already stormed it, taken it hostage. Now he was in a position to break it. And she couldn't prepare herself because she wasn't sure quite how it would happen.

He didn't seem to want to hurt her. But the fact was that he would be leaving in a few days, going back to a life that didn't—couldn't—include her. That knowledge alone was enough to make her heart ache.

She drained her wineglass, then looked at it quizzically. "My head's beginning to spin," she said, avoiding his question. "I think I've had more than enough of this."

"Can you stay with me tonight?"

Carly set her glass on the nightstand, then laid her fork on the plate. "I have to leave early," she said, implicitly agreeing. "I do rounds at the hospital even on Saturday mornings."

"Do you need to call your grandmother?"

Her smile felt strangely shy, considering their earlier decadence. "I told her not to wait up."

He moved the plate out of their way, setting his empty glass beside Carly's. "I like a woman who plans ahead."

"Let's just say I like to be prepared for any contingency."

Including heartache? Could she ever really be prepared for that? She couldn't answer her own questions, didn't want to face them now. She cooperated fully when Alex tugged her back into his arms.

"Carly?"

"Mmm?" She was almost asleep. She couldn't see the clock, but she guessed that the time had to be close to 2:00 a.m. She could almost hear morning tiptoeing toward the cabin, bringing an end to this long, delightful night.

Alex's voice was a deep rumble from the darkness in the bedroom. He lay close beside her, his legs entwined with hers, his arm pillowing her head. "I don't want it to end when I go back to Boston."

Her eyes flew open at that. "I—"

"You've become very special to me. This isn't just a vacation affair—it never was."

"Boston's a long way from here," she murmured, wondering what, exactly, he had in mind, even as she thrilled at the sincerity of his words.

"That's why we have telephones and airplanes and E-mail."

Carly winced. "A long-distance relationship. I've heard they never work."

"We could give it a try. I don't want to leave Tuesday without knowing that I'll be talking to you again. Seeing you again."

She felt doubt creeping in beneath the pleasure that he wanted to maintain contact with her. "We're both very busy people, Alex. You said yourself that this is the first vacation you've had in years. And I haven't really had one since I bought the clinic five years ago—not for more than a day or two at a time. How—"

"We'll work something out," he cut in. "Just don't close the door, Carly. Say you'll give it a try."

"I won't refuse your calls," she said, her mixed emotions making her tone wry.

"Well, that's a start, I suppose," he murmured, equally ironic.

Biting her lip, Carly closed her eyes and snuggled more deeply into the bedclothes. She needed sleep. Her mind needed to be clear when they had this conversation. At the moment, lying in Alex's arms, she couldn't think of any reason why they *couldn't* maintain a long-distance relationship.

After Carly's hospital rounds Saturday morning, she and Alex drove Betty to Little Rock to visit Bob in the hospital, where he would remain for two or three more days. They found Debbie sitting by his bed, fussing at him about something. Bob looked perfectly content to listen to her complaints. Probably, Carly suspected, because he was aware of the new note of tenderness behind Debbie's usually gruff tone.

Bob was still sore and weak from his surgery but announced that he was more than ready to get home. He'd been up for a while that afternoon, and he declared himself well on the road to recovery. He thanked Alex again for saving his life. Alex accepted the thanks graciously, then quickly changed the subject, assuring Bob that he would soon be caving again, as long as he followed his doctors' orders and took good care of himself.

''He'll do that,'' Debbie said flatly, sounding prepared to stand over Bob to make sure. Carly had no doubt that she meant just that. Debbie and Bob still had some differences to overcome, but they seemed to be working in that direction.

Carly glanced surreptitiously at Alex, wondering what the odds were that the two of *them* would be able to maintain a fulfilling relationship with the distance and differences they faced.

Alex took Carly and Betty out for an early dinner in a very nice Italian restaurant before they left Little Rock to begin the long drive home. They lingered over pasta and conversation, and Carly was struck again by how very well her grandmother and Alex got along. He had certainly made an impression during the short time he'd been with them.

It was very late by the time they got to Carly's house. Alex didn't stay long. Wistfully, Carly watched him drive away.

Two more days.

It was inevitable, of course, that Tuesday arrived. It dawned rainy and cool, a presage of the winter that wasn't really very far away. Carly crossed her arms and stared morosely out the window, thinking that the fates were being very uncreative to settle for such clichéd weather on an already depressing day.

Alex's hands settled on her shoulders, drawing her backward against his bare chest. She felt him kiss the top of her head.

"Good morning." His voice was still gruff from sleep.

She leaned back against him. "Good morning."

"It's early."

"Just before six," she agreed. "I have to be at the hospital at eight."

"Are you going to wear this very fetching outfit?"

She smiled a little. She was wearing nothing but Alex's denim shirt, which hung to the middle of her thighs. "I'd better not."

"Too bad. I know seeing you like this would make *me* feel better, if I were the one lying in a hospital bed."

"I think my patients would prefer that I look a bit more professional."

"That's just as well, I suppose. I rather like being the only one who sees you like this." He fell silent then, and Carly wondered if he was thinking the same thing she was. Would it be the last time he would see her like this?

"Since you won't be needing this shirt today..." From behind her, he found the top button and slid it out of its hole.

"Oh, do you want it back?" Already the now familiar excitement was coursing through her, causing her skin to tingle, her limbs to grow heavy, her breathing to accelerate.

It only took a touch of Alex's hand to do this to her. She couldn't imagine that anyone else would ever affect her this way, now that she'd been with Alex. A moment later, the shirt slid off her shoulders and fell to the floor. Once he'd removed it from her, he showed no more interest in the garment. To her delight, Carly was the sole focus of his attentions.

She turned in his arms and wrapped her own around his neck. "Make love to me, Alex," she murmured, rising on tiptoe to whisper the words against his mouth.

One last time.

She'd added that phrase silently, but he must have heard it. His arms were possessive when he dragged her against him, his kiss fierce. And when he drew her down to the bed and buried himself inside her, she felt as if she had been thoroughly, irrefutably claimed.

Alex walked Carly to her truck with just enough time remaining for her to make it to the hospital by eight. He held her hand during the brief walk and found himself unwilling to release it when they reached the driver's side door.

With a sigh, he looked down at their intertwined

fingers, then lifted her hand to his lips. "I don't want to let go," he murmured.

Her fingers tightened around his. "Neither do I."

"I'll miss you."

He watched as she moistened her lips. Her chocolate brown eyes were dry but overly bright when she looked up at him. "I'll miss you, too."

"You'll take care of yourself, along with all these other people you take care of?"

She nodded. "Yes."

A drop of rain fell from the heavy clouds overhead, landing on Carly's cheek, tracing downward like a solitary tear. Alex used his free hand to wipe the drop away with his thumb.

"You'd better go," he said reluctantly. "It's starting to rain, and you don't want to be late for your rounds."

She nodded, her face devoid of expression now. "Have a good flight home, Alex."

Home. He thought of the impeccably decorated apartment waiting for him in Boston. The busy schedule he would return to the very next day. Patients, consultations, meetings, long-planned social engagements.

Would there be any moment during those hectic days that he would not think of Carly?

He leaned over to kiss her. She responded for a heartbeat, then quickly pulled away. "I'd better go," she whispered, and climbed quickly behind the wheel of her truck.

Alex watched her as she drove away.

Another drop of rain hit him in the face.

He glanced up at the bleak clouds. "Very funny,"

he muttered. And then he turned and walked back into the fishing cabin. He had to finish packing.

Carly was proud of herself for not crying. She would have been humiliated to stand there blubbering like a frustrated child or—even worse—following her instincts and latching onto his arm, begging him not to go.

Perhaps she could have handled the farewell a bit better—a bit less stiffly—but she'd been calm, collected and dignified about it. All a total facade, of course.

Already she was wondering when he would call, when she would hear his voice again. She was thinking of the beautiful women she'd seen with him in that magazine article and wondering if any of them would be waiting with open arms to greet him.

Already she missed him so badly she ached with it. But at least she hadn't cried in front of him, she thought, clinging to her pride with metaphorical fingernails. And then she reached up a hand to wipe away the tears that had escaped the moment she was alone.

Fourteen

"So, Alex. How was Arkansas?"

Two weeks after returning from his vacation, Alex forced a smile for the older colleague who'd asked the question. "Fine, Mark. Great fishing. Beautiful scenery. You should go there sometime."

"Me?" The urbane, wealthy plastic surgeon chuckled. "I prefer to go somewhere a bit more civilized when I vacation. Someplace where the locals wear shoes," he added, glancing smugly down at the soft Italian leather enclosing his own feet.

Alex's smile faded. "I wore shoes the entire time I was there. And so did the 'locals.'"

The attractive dermatologist at Mark's side eyed Alex curiously. "Hard to imagine you doing nothing but fishing for two solid weeks, Alex. Did you have a chance to take in some of the local flavor? Meet any of the people?"

Alex nodded. "I made some friends. Attended a charity dance. Visited the county hospital."

Lisa's neatly arched eyebrows rose. "A little county hospital in rural Arkansas? Was it as primitive as it sounds?"

Alex thought of the medical facilities available to the physicians mingling at this hospital-sponsored reception. In comparison, Carly's little hospital *was* a bit primitive. The equipment was hardly state-of-the-art, and the lack of money available for salaries probably made it difficult to attract and keep staff. He couldn't imagine either Mark or Lisa being content to practice there without the very generous compensation, impressive facilities and social prestige they had become accustomed to. And yet...

"The patients I saw were receiving more than adequate care," he said, couching his answer carefully and yet honestly.

"I have an old friend who works in a hospital in rural Mississippi," Mark commented. "He says it's like practicing in a third world country. The hours he has to work are unbelievable—he's on call twenty-four hours a day, seven days a week—and the conditions are stark, to say the least. His patients are too poor and undereducated to take care of their health, so he's constantly dealing with late-stage medical emergencies. And he doesn't make as much in a year as I pull down in a matter of months. I wouldn't trade places with him for anything."

Alex didn't doubt that for a minute. Mark made little secret of the fact that he'd gone into medicine more for the money and the prestige than from any higher calling. Alex had been asking himself lately whether his own reasons had been any more noble.

"The doctors I met there seemed to enjoy their work," he said a bit lamely.

Lisa waved her hand like a fan in front of her face. "So what did y'all learn while y'all were down there in the South?"

"I learned that the word 'y'all' is plural," Alex answered a bit shortly. "Excuse me, but Dr. Melsmith is signaling me." He could almost feel Mark's and

Lisa's gazes on the back of his neck as he walked away.

Damn, but he missed Carly.

Carly missed Alex.

Three weeks after she'd driven away from him, she still ached every time she thought of him—which, she could admit to herself, was all the time. No matter how busy she stayed, no matter how intently she concentrated on her work, her family or her friends, thoughts of Alex were always at the back of her mind.

He called. Several times a week. They talked for hours. But it wasn't enough. And the conversations were becoming more difficult, more stilted as distance and differences lay so heavily between them.

Carly predicted that the calls would soon come less often and then would eventually stop altogether when neither of them could think of anything else to say.

"I need to see you, Carly," Alex told her on the phone that evening. "I miss you."

"I miss you, too," she replied. "But..."

"Surely you can arrange a few days off. I managed to take two weeks. Can't you take at least a long weekend?"

She could probably arrange a long weekend. Her grandmother would be fine for a few days, and Dr. Gresham would take her emergency calls, if Carly promised to return the favor sometime.

But would it really be a wise move?

She wanted to see Alex again. Wanted it so badly she could almost taste it. She wanted to see where he lived, where he worked. She wanted to meet his friends. To make love with him.

But if it hurt this badly to be apart from him after

spending only two short weeks with him, how badly would she feel after saying goodbye to him once again?

"Carly?" His voice was deep. Enticing. "Will you come to Boston?"

"I'll see what I can do," she promised, knowing she didn't have the willpower to turn him down. Not when she wanted so badly to say yes. "When would be the best time for me to come?"

"Anytime," he answered promptly. "If I have any plans, I'll cancel them. I want to be with you."

"I'll see what I can do," she repeated weakly.

"Just let me know when you'll be here." He sounded as if he had no doubt that she would make the arrangements.

They talked only a few more minutes, then Carly hung up the phone. She had to collect herself before she could rejoin her grandmother in the living room.

"Was that Alex?" Betty asked, looking away from the TV-tabloid news program she had been watching.

Carly nodded and curled into her favorite big chair. "He sent his regards to you."

"He's such a dear." Betty studied Carly's face for a moment, then asked, "Is something wrong, Carly? Did you and Alex have a disagreement?"

Carly shook her head. "Of course not. We had a very nice conversation."

"You look so serious. Are you sure nothing's bothering you?"

Plucking at a string on her slacks, Carly shrugged. "Alex wants me to go to Boston to visit him for a long weekend."

Betty considered it for a moment, then nodded.

"You should go. You deserve a few days off occasionally."

Carly continued to pluck at the spot where the loose thread had been. "It isn't easy for me to get away from here. I can't just drop everything to go running off to Boston."

"One day away from your clinic," Betty said dismissively. "One weekend away from the telephone. I think we'll all survive without you for two or three days, Carly."

"I couldn't go next weekend. I have that staff thing at the hospital Saturday afternoon. I really should be there."

"So go the next weekend."

"That's the second weekend of November. We're having the health fair at the high school. I can't miss that. And the weekend after that is Thanksgiving. The whole family's going to be here."

"After that you get into the Christmas season and you'll be too busy to get away.... Carly, do you *want* to go to Boston?"

Carly's fingers fell still. "I want to see Alex," she whispered. "But..."

"You don't want to see him *there*. In his own life."

Her eyes widening, Carly looked up at her grandmother. "I hadn't thought of it that way. But I think you're right."

"Because you're afraid he'll look different to you there. That he won't be the Alex you knew here. You'll see firsthand that he has a life that doesn't include you."

Swallowing hard, Carly nodded. "All of that is true, I suppose. You're spooky sometimes, Granny."

Betty's smile was bittersweet. "I simply know my granddaughter."

"So what should I do?" It wasn't the first time Carly had turned to her grandmother for answers; she doubted that it would be the last.

"Go to Boston, dear. It's the only way you'll ever know."

"Know what?" Carly asked warily.

"Whether you and Alex have a chance to make this work out. Isn't it better to know sooner than later?"

Carly sighed. "You're probably right."

Betty apparently decided she'd said enough for now. She turned her attention back to the television, but Carly was aware of the slightly worried looks her grandmother gave her during the remainder of the evening.

It was the first weekend in December when Carly finally made it to Boston. She arrived early Thursday evening and would not return home until Sunday.

It had been two months since she'd last seen Alex, and she was extremely nervous as she walked off the airplane. Alex had implied that he had not been with another woman since he'd left Carly, and she believed him. She'd made it clear enough in return that there were no other men in her life. The long telephone calls had continued, when time allowed for both of them, and they still talked easily enough, but actually seeing each other was different.

What if he saw her in an entirely different light now that he'd been back in his own world for so long, among the beautiful, sophisticated women in his own social circles? What if he no longer found Carly attractive, or even particularly interesting?

She knew nothing about high society; what if she embarrassed herself or—even worse—Alex?

What if *he* was different in his own setting? What if Carly didn't like him here? What if she found him stuffy or snobbish or pretentious or cold? It had been so long since she'd seen him, she had trouble even picturing him clearly. What if the magic they'd felt before had been only a fleeting phenomenon?

And then he was there, standing in front of her. Smiling. And her eyes filled with tears.

He took a step toward her, holding a single red rose in one hand. He held out his arms. Carly dropped her carry-on bag and stepped into his embrace. Oddly enough, she felt as though she'd just come home.

Carly had been to medical conferences in Manhattan and Chicago, so this wasn't her first experience with a large city. Boston, of course, had a flavor of its own. Not that Carly paid much attention to local flavor. Her attention was focused almost solely on Alex.

In the living room of the impeccably decorated penthouse apartment he'd brought her to, she made him stand still as she walked slowly around him. The jeans and denim shirts he'd worn in Arkansas had been exchanged for beautifully tailored wool slacks and a discreetly monogrammed dress shirt. His hand-knit fisherman's sweater alone had probably cost as much as Carly's entire outfit—shoes, purse, coat, underwear and all.

He looked entirely at home in the expensive clothes and the elegant surroundings. She couldn't imagine the man standing in front of her now ever crawling through that muddy cave in Missouri. Had she seen him first this way, it would have come as no surprise to her to learn that he was a noted physician and a magazine heartthrob.

''Well?'' he asked when she'd made a full circle around him. ''Do I pass inspection?''

She smiled a bit wistfully. ''You look like Dr. Robert Alexander Keating of Boston.''

His quick frown let her know that he understood her meaning. ''I'm still just Alex. The same guy you knew before.''

Just Alex? No. There was a great deal more to him than that.

''Carly.'' He reached out to take her hands and pull her toward him. ''Look at me and tell me you don't know me.''

She looked into his eyes, saw herself reflected there. And she saw the man she'd fallen in love with, still there beneath the expensive clothes and successful facade. ''I know the part of you that you've shown me, Alex. But even you have to admit you're different here.''

He looked as though he might argue. And then he hesitated, grimaced and admitted, ''There's probably some truth to that.''

She glanced expressively again at his clothing, his cappuccino-and-cream living room decor, the expensive artwork on his textured walls. She could think of nothing to say in response to his obvious statement.

Still holding her hands, he pulled her closer. ''I want you to know me, Carly. I want you to know me better than anyone else ever has. Better than anyone ever could.''

"I want that, too," she assured him, her throat tight. "Oh, Alex, I've missed you..."

He smothered the words beneath his mouth, letting her know that he'd missed her, too.

Alex seemed determined to introduce Carly to every aspect of his life in the short time she would be staying with him. They dined at an elegant new Boston restaurant Thursday evening, where several of his acquaintances greeted him, eyeing Carly with discreet curiosity. Alex introduced her as his "special friend from Arkansas, Dr. Carly Fletcher," making no effort to hide his intense interest in her.

On Friday, Carly accompanied Alex to his offices, which were located on the tenth floor of a medical services building connected to the hospital where he practiced. The university hospital system in which Carly had trained in Little Rock was well equipped and well respected, but she couldn't help being impressed by the facilities Alex had at his disposal, particularly when she compared them to her small clinic and the modest little county hospital at home.

Carly could appreciate the technology she was seeing, but she had no desire to trade places with anyone there. Not that any of the doctors she met would have believed that, judging from the comments they made.

"A family practice in rural Arkansas?" one of the younger doctors said with a barely concealed shudder. "Did you get into one of those slave-labor contracts to pay off medical school, or what?"

"No," Carly answered simply. "I practice there because I want to."

"I see. Well, I have a friend who works at a free health clinic in Harlem. I never understood why she wanted to do that, either, but I suppose someone has to take care of those patients."

"Sorry about that," Alex murmured when the other doctor had moved out of hearing. "Not all the doctors around here have that attitude, I assure you."

Carly shrugged. "There are jerks in every profession," she answered bluntly. "I don't let them bother me."

She met a few others that day who lifted an eyebrow when they heard her accent and who treated her rather condescendingly, but most of the people Alex introduced her to were quite gracious. She particularly enjoyed meeting a couple of his patients. She could see that they regarded him with near awe, treating him with the respect one would have thought reserved for a head of state.

In return, Alex was professional, polite, a bit reserved, somewhat formal. Hardly the casual, cozy, easy camaraderie Carly maintained with her own patients, but then Alex's practice was different, she reminded herself. He was a specialist, not a primary care physician.

He would see some of his patients only a time or two, hardly time to get to know them on a personal basis. Carly, on the other hand, knew her patients as friends and neighbors. She delivered their babies, treated their children's runny noses, set their broken bones, cried with them when death inevitably took its toll. Her patients did not hold her in awe and reverence, though she believed they respected her. But she liked to think that they also liked her, that many of them even loved her, just as she liked and loved them in return.

That evening, Alex took her to a social function at

his country club. Feeling self-conscious in the expensively cut, rarely worn black dress she'd brought with her for such an occasion, she stayed close to his side as he introduced her to his social acquaintances. While she heard a few comments about her Southern accent and was asked a few tactless questions about her home state, she was treated pleasantly enough. She cynically suspected that being a physician—even a simple country doctor—gave her a certain credibility. Had she been a teacher or a dress-shop clerk, she might not have been treated quite so cordially.

Of course, it didn't hurt her status to be seen on the arm of Dr. Robert Alexander Keating, she reminded herself even more cynically.

Alex felt almost absurdly proud to be at Carly's side that evening. She looked so beautiful, he thought, admiring her openly. Not supermodel beautiful, perhaps. She wasn't the youngest, thinnest, tallest or most fashionable woman in the room. But to Alex, she was the most appealing.

Her makeup, as usual, was lightly applied. Her brown eyes sparkled with intelligence and her own warm, vibrant personality. Her dark blond hair had been pinned up, baring her slender neck and the smooth, creamy shoulders revealed by the sleeveless black dress that skimmed her figure. She was obviously in excellent physical condition, but not so painfully thin that a puff of air would blow her over. Alex wouldn't have changed one thing about her.

Within less than two hours of their arrival, Carly had worked her magic on many of Alex's acquaintances, who seemed taken with her natural warmth, humor and charm. She had a way of listening to someone with her full concentration, looking very interested, asking questions that proved she was listening closely. People liked that personal attention, Alex mused, knowing that was part of Carly's talent as a family practice doctor.

Her humor was gentle, artfully self-deprecating and yet dignified, her pride in her Southern roots unmistakable, even as she shared a laugh at some of the stereotypes Bostonians held about the South. She could talk comfortably about medicine, politics and current affairs, and while she admitted that her busy schedule made it difficult for her to keep up with current movies and bestsellers, she was obviously well read and well educated.

Alex suspected that she was completely unaware of the spell she was weaving among his friends. And he found her natural modesty delightful, as well.

He loved her with all his being. He'd suspected it for a long time and had realized that he was *in* love with her before he left Arkansas, but the depth of his feeling for her had crystallized for him when she'd stepped off the plane the day before. He could hardly bear to think of watching her get on another plane to fly out of his life once again.

He wanted her to stay with him. Permanently.

With mental apologies to her friends and patients back home in Arkansas, he intended to do everything within his power to convince her to leave the home she'd made for herself there, the home she loved so deeply, and make a new home with Alex.

It wasn't an easy task he'd given himself. But nothing Alex had ever done had been more important to him than this.

He waited until they were in bed that evening, their bodies still limp and damp, their hearts still racing from the most spectacular lovemaking they'd shared yet. He had to wait a moment to recover his voice before he could speak coherently.

"I love you, Carly."

She went so still that he thought even her breathing might have been suspended for at least a moment or two.

"Carly?" Was she really so surprised to hear him say the words after he'd just made every effort to show her what he felt for her? "Did you hear me?"

"I heard you," she said after a moment. "I was just...I wasn't expecting it."

Not exactly the answer he'd hoped for. "Well?" he asked, uncharacteristically insecure. "Don't you have anything to say in return?"

The lengthy pause that followed seemed like one of the longest intervals of Alex's life. No woman had ever metaphorically held his heart in her hands before. He hadn't realized quite how badly it would hurt.

"Is it really that hard to answer?" he asked, rising on one elbow to look down at her as she lay against the pillow, biting her lip and looking worried.

She sighed. "No, not really. I'm just...not sure what will happen afterward."

"Can you tell me what you feel?" He wanted the most important issue settled first.

"I love you, Alex. I knew that before you ever left Arkansas."

He felt his heart start to beat again, still a bit painfully, but with renewed hope and determination. He leaned over to kiss her, a kiss made even more special than the ones that preceded it because they both knew now that it was given in love.

His first instinct was to use her words to bind her to him, to catch her in this moment of weakness and demand promises, unbreakable vows. She loved him. She'd said she did, and he believed her. How could she even think about leaving him now?

But Alex had always understood the concept of timing, and this wasn't the right time to talk about the future. He must content himself for now with the knowledge that Carly returned his love.

He had tomorrow to press his case with her. And he intended to make good use of that time.

Fifteen

No professional tour guide had ever given a more enthusiastic view of the city than Alex provided Carly on Saturday. Perhaps it was a rambling and somewhat disorganized tour, but Alex made sure Carly saw everything she had ever wanted to see in Boston.

They began at Boston Common, the fifty-acre public park, which, Alex explained, was usually filled with tourists, sunworshipers, sidewalk performers, hustlers and outspoken demonstrators in the summer. On this beautiful, pleasantly mild, early winter morning, the crowds were light, though Carly had no problem imagining the park filled almost to capacity with people.

She drank in the historic sites she'd only read about before—Paul Revere's home, the Old North Church, Faneuil Hall and Quincy Market. To someone from the relatively new state of Arkansas, it was the age of the buildings in Boston that impressed her the most. As Alex said, only in Boston could a building constructed in 1798 still be referred to as the "New State House."

Carly looked up at the golden dome of the building in question and said, "Elvie Haney's house back home was built in 1920-something. That's the oldest occupied house I can think of in Seventy-Six, though there are a couple of foundations still around from houses in the 1800s. You know why our town is called Seventy-Six, don't you?"

"I kept meaning to ask that while I was there."

"Legend has it that when it was officially incorporated in 1876, an official count was taken of the residents. Turned out there were exactly seventy-six citizens of the new little town."

"Hence, the name of Seventy-Six," Alex concluded with a chuckle.

"Mmm-hmm. Just imagine, your 'new' State House was almost a hundred years old when my town came into existence."

They had lunch in Chinatown, a neighborhood Carly found absolutely fascinating. They paused for a while beside the lovely, utterly peaceful reflecting pool outside the Christian Science Center in the business district. They climbed the two hundred ninety-four steps inside the towering granite obelisk of the Bunker Hill Monument, finding a breathtaking view of Boston at the top, where they rested and regained their breath. They had afternoon cappuccinos at a delightful café in the Italian North End, and then walked to the Charlestown Navy Yard to admire the USS *Constitution*, "Old Ironsides."

Alex drove her into Cambridge to show her the campus of his alma mater, Harvard University, and the Harvard University Medical School. The sun had set by then, and the streets and buildings glittered with recently hung Christmas lights and decorations. Carly thought it was all beautiful.

He took her back to Boston for a seafood dinner in an elegant, yet casual restaurant near the Harbor. They completed the day at a cozy, noisy Irish pub where Alex was greeted as a regular and Carly as a welcomed visitor. Not once did Alex's pager intrude, nor did thoughts of patients, responsibilities, differences or coming separations.

Carly had an absolutely marvelous time.

It was very late by the time they returned to Alex's apartment. Carly was tired, bemused and perhaps a little giddy from the single Irish whiskey she had allowed herself at the pub.

She turned into Alex's arms when he closed the door behind them, looping her own around his neck. "I had a wonderful day. Thank you, Alex."

He pulled her close and kissed her with the new tenderness she had noted since they'd exchanged vows of love. "I love you, Carly."

It wasn't the first time he'd told her that day. He'd murmured the words several times, as if to remind her that he hadn't forgotten what he'd said during the night, or what she had said in return. Every time she heard the words, she reacted again with a shivery mixture of joy, incredulity, excitement and a touch of sheer panic. "I love you, too."

He smiled down at her and reached up to brush a strand of hair from her cheek. "I enjoyed showing you my city today. I've never had such a good time playing tour guide. I'm only sorry that we couldn't spend more time at each of the sites we visited, so that you could have gotten a more thorough overview of them. We only touched on the historical artifacts and exhibits, for example."

Carly nodded. "I know. But I preferred seeing a little of everything rather than spending a lot of time in one place…at least on this trip."

She was acknowledging that there would be other trips. Though she'd tried not to think about the future during the past few hours, she assumed that being in love meant to Alex, as it did to her, that there would be a continuing relationship. More visits, phone calls, rare vacations...stolen moments together whenever possible. Not the most satisfying of relationships, perhaps, but workable—for a while, at least.

Alex hesitated a moment, then reached up to remove her arms from around his neck, keeping her hands in his. "Let's sit down and talk, Carly. Would you like some coffee?"

She shook her head. "No. What do you want to talk about?"

He drew her to a low couch and settled on the cushions beside her. "You like Boston. I could see it on your face today."

"It's a fascinating place," she admitted. "Like any big city, it has its share of problems, but I can see why people like living here. And I certainly understand why you enjoy practicing medicine here. The facilities at your disposal are...well, they're mind-boggling."

"Yes, they are," he admitted. "And yet we also have a large population who can't afford access to the best medical care. Desperately poor urban areas where good doctors are hard to attract and to keep."

She nodded, thinking of the free health clinics Alex had pointed out during their necessarily abbreviated tour of his city. The abject urban poverty so painfully obvious in some of the neighborhoods he'd driven her through. She had heard both from Alex and, in more detail, from his devoted staff that Alex gave a great deal to those communities, both in time and money, though his practice was primarily based in the hospital setting.

Alex seemed to take a deep breath before saying, "You could practice here, Carly. The kind of medicine you enjoy, primary care. With your talent for getting to know people, for earning their trust and their confidences, you'd be a valuable asset to the public health organizations here."

Her breath caught. Surely he wasn't suggesting…

"I'm asking you to stay here with me," he said, making it very clear exactly what he was suggesting. "I don't want a long-distance relationship. I want us to be together. Carly, I'm asking you to marry me."

Quick panic threatened to smother her. She shook her head, tugging at her hands, which he refused to release. "Alex, I…"

"I know you're thinking about your grandmother," he said quickly—and not entirely accurately. "She can come with you, live with us. We'll get a house big enough for all three of us…big enough for a child or two, as well. You once said you would love to have children, and so would I—as long as it's with you."

Oh, this was unfair. The thought of having a child with Alex was something she wanted so badly she ached with it.

"I don't know what to say." She would have rubbed her temples if he had released her hands to allow her to do so. She shouldn't have had that drink at the pub, she thought dazedly. She really wasn't a drinker.

"I've caught you off guard." His expression held both understanding and apology.

"You could say that," Carly agreed dryly.

He'd asked her to marry him. She couldn't have

been much more surprised if he'd suddenly sprouted wings.

He lifted her hands to his lips. "You need time to think."

She seized the reprieve gratefully. "Yes. I need time."

"You can give me your answer in the morning."

"In the *morning?*" He considered that giving her time to think?

"I'd like to have this settled before you get on that plane tomorrow. Knowing you'll be back to stay is the only way I'll be able to watch you leave."

She couldn't help noticing that he seemed awfully confident about what her answer would be.

"Carly, I love you."

A faint sigh escaped her. "I love you, too. But..."

"But you need to think. And rest," he finished for her. He stood and drew her to her feet. "Let's go to bed."

Carly got very little rest that night. But she did a great deal of thinking. And by the time morning dawned, she knew what she had to do.

Alex gave her time to shower, dress and have breakfast, though she had little appetite. She was finishing her second cup of coffee when his patience ran out.

"Carly?"

He didn't have to say more. She knew exactly what he was asking.

And she gave him the only answer she could. "I love you, Alex," she said, her throat tight. "But I can't marry you."

He looked stunned. "Why?" he asked simply.

"Boston is your world, not mine. I don't belong here."

"You could make a place for yourself here." His tone had taken on a new urgency, and his navy eyes gleamed with determination.

He wouldn't take her refusal easily, she could see. She moistened her lips and tried to think of the words that would help him understand. "Alex, I grew up in Arkansas. I received my education and my medical training there. My family and my friends are there. I've never wanted to live or work anywhere else. Can you understand that?"

He shook his head, deliberately stubborn, she suspected. "You're talking geography. People are people, Carly. There are poor patients here who need you as badly as the ones you treat in Arkansas."

"I'm needed at home. And that's where I need to be."

"Your patients could find another doctor to replace you."

"Of course. But don't you understand? I don't want them to replace me. That's *my* clinic. Those are *my* patients. It's my home. And I can't leave it."

"You mean you won't leave it."

She thought about it a moment, then nodded. "Yes, I suppose that's what I'm saying. It's taken me a long time, a lot of work and a great deal of hard-earned money to build my practice. I'm not willing to walk away from it now, not when I'm needed so badly there."

Alex's voice was gruff with frustration. "And what about your personal needs? Love? Children?"

She had to force her voice to remain steady. "I'm thirty-four years old. I accepted some time ago that I may never have children. I knew when I went into medicine that it took a full commitment, long hours and total dedication. I have women friends who are both doctors and mothers, but it's difficult. If it turns out that it never happens for me, I still have to believe that I made the right choice. I love my work, my patients, my home."

"And me?"

"And you," she added steadily. "I can't deny that."

"But you're making your choice. And I lose."

A single tear escaped her. "I'm sorry if you see it that way. I only know that I can't move here. I just can't, Alex. It isn't where I belong."

She saw the acceptance slowly appear in his eyes. "There's nothing I can say to change your mind, is there?"

"No," she whispered. "I'm sorry. I wish things were different. But I could never be truly happy if I walk away from what I know is right for me."

"You're turning me down." Alex sounded as though he could hardly believe his ears.

She sat silently, unable to repeat her answer. Turning Alex down was probably the hardest thing she'd ever done. But she'd lain awake half the night thinking about what he'd asked of her, trying to imagine herself leaving her home and her practice and starting over here, where she would be only one doctor among so many. When she'd slept, she'd dreamed of home...the trees and hills, the rivers and lakes. Her friends.

As much as she loved Alex, she knew they could never be truly happy together as long as part of her heart lay elsewhere.

Alex looked down at his coffee cup, his expression suddenly blank. "Where do we go now?" he asked, his voice rather flat.

She swallowed. This was the hardest part of all. "You take me to the airport. And then...we say goodbye."

His eyes lifted slowly to her face. "You mean that literally."

It wasn't a question.

She nodded. "I've thought about this, too, Alex. How long would either of us be satisfied with telephone calls and rare weekend visits? You want—and deserve—more than that, and yet it's all I can offer. I have a life in Arkansas, you have a life here. We have to go on with them."

"This is really what you want, Carly?"

"No," she said with a sigh. "It's what has to be."

He sat in silence for several long, unhappy minutes. "You never mentioned the alternative to my request," he said eventually.

She moistened her lips. "What alternative?"

"I could move to Arkansas."

She had to admit to herself that the thought had crossed her mind—only to be immediately rejected. She could no more picture Dr. Robert Alexander Keating setting up a practice in rural Arkansas than she could see herself moving to Boston.

She'd known all along that they came from different worlds. She had simply deluded herself for a while that the differences weren't important.

"You have a life here, Alex," she repeated quietly. "I would never ask you to leave it."

His face could have been carved from marble as he studied her, his shuttered eyes searching her face. And then he pushed himself to his feet. "I'll help you pack."

She'd hurt him, she thought, taking no offense at his curt tone. She'd worried so much about being hurt herself that she hadn't quite realized she held the power to hurt Alex in return.

Turning him down had broken her heart.

Hurting him shattered it.

Not trusting herself to speak without bursting into tears—or promising him whatever he wanted from her, whether it was best for her or not—she bit her lip and nodded. It was time for Carly to go home.

They said very little during the drive to the airport. There was very little to say.

Carly spent most of the ride looking out the passenger window. She couldn't bear to look at Alex. The Christmas decorations she saw along the way only depressed her further. She didn't imagine that this would be the happiest holiday she'd ever spent. Not even Santa Claus could bring Carly what she wanted most this year.

They arrived at the airport a full hour before her flight was to leave.

"I don't want you to stay," she said to Alex after checking her bags. "I'll read at the gate until my plane boards."

He looked as if he wanted to argue, but he merely nodded. "If that's what you want."

It was the only way she could think of to preserve her dignity for the next hour. She drew a deep breath. "I don't know how to say goodbye."

"Then don't."

She tried to smile. "Okay. I won't."

Alex drew a deep breath, ignoring the bustle of the

airport around them. His voice was quiet, yet she had no trouble hearing him over the other noise. "I had a great time, Carly."

She knew he wasn't just talking about the past few days. "So did I," she whispered.

He touched her cheek. "Take care of yourself, Doc."

Her smile wavered, but she was able to hold on to it. "You, too, Doc."

His kiss was tender. Sad. She watched him walk away through a shimmering curtain of tears.

On a Thursday evening in early March, Carly sat on her porch, huddled into a warm jacket, rocking and gazing at the stars. Across the street, Francis barked a greeting to her before returning his attention to the fresh food in his bowl. Bob had just fed the dog, waving and calling a greeting to Carly as he'd done so. He had seemed to understand that she needed to be alone for a while, so he had simply gone back into his house after taking care of Francis.

Bob had recovered nicely from his heart surgery. Though his condition was still being closely monitored, there was no reason to believe he wouldn't live a long, normal life. He and Debbie were openly dating now, and Bob was giving Debbie plenty of time to get used to the idea of marrying a minister. Carly thought it wouldn't be long before Debbie decided that it wasn't nearly as daunting a prospect as she'd once believed.

Carly tried to find comfort in the thought that her friends seemed happy, but it wasn't easy just then. She'd had a rough day. It had begun before dawn, when she'd been called to the hospital to deliver a baby who'd been in a hurry to be born. She still remembered cradling that tiny boy in her arms for an extra moment before passing him to the waiting nurse. She still felt the sharp pang of regret that she would never have a child of her own.

She'd ended her workday by telling a devastated man that she suspected his wife of forty-five years had cancer. She'd referred the couple to a top-rated oncologist in Little Rock, but she was afraid there would be little the prominent specialist could do. The woman had waited too long to see about her symptoms because she'd worried that she couldn't afford medical care.

Her delay had cost her—and her family—much more.

Carly had never once regretted her choice of professions. But tonight, more than usual, she was keenly aware of how heavily it sometimes weighed on her.

She didn't allow herself to cry often—either over her job or the constant heartache that was still very much with her—but she felt like crying tonight. She was afraid to start for fear that she wouldn't be able to stop.

"Carly?" Her grandmother spoke from the doorway.

Carly turned her head. "What is it, Granny?"

Betty held out a cordless telephone receiver. "You have a call."

Biting back a groan, Carly reached for the phone and tried to find the strength to go back into doctor mode. "Thank you," she said, and took the phone.

Her grandmother studied her for a moment with a hard-to-read expression, then nodded firmly and moved back inside. "I'll leave you to your privacy."

Carly lifted the phone to her ear. "Dr. Fletcher."

"I'm hurting bad, Doc. I need you."

It had been almost three months since she'd heard his voice. She recognized it immediately.

"Alex," she whispered, feeling her limbs go weak with shock.

"Just answer one question for me. Do you still love me?"

"Yes," she said on a sigh. "That hasn't changed. But—"

"That's all I needed to hear," he said. And disconnected the call.

Bewildered, Carly looked blankly at the buzzing receiver in her hand. What on earth...?

A car turned into her driveway. A tall, dark-haired man stepped out. His face was obscured by nighttime shadows, but Carly knew him.

The telephone hit the porch with a crash.

A moment later, Carly was in Alex's arms.

She spoke breathlessly, her words broken by hot, hungry kisses. "You should have told me you were... I missed you so much... You shouldn't have come... I'm so glad to see you... You should have stayed away... I'm so happy you're here."

If Alex was confused by her rambling contradictions, he didn't let it show. He held her so tightly her ribs were compressed, and he was kissing her every time he could catch her mouth.

"You said you couldn't ask me to give up my life in Boston," he murmured against her lips. "You didn't seem to understand how badly I wanted you to ask. I couldn't wait any longer."

She caught his face between her hands, noting that

his skin was cool and yet somehow hot at the same time. "Alex, what are you saying?"

"You said you'd been thinking about taking on a partner," he reminded her. "One who speaks Spanish fluently, as I remember. I'm applying for the job. I specialize in cardiac care, by the way," he added with a faint smile.

"I—" Stunned, she stared up at him. "You want to move here?"

He nodded. "How do you feel about building a new clinic? Maybe adding a couple more doctors? My research indicates that this area is developing fast. There's a growing need for bigger and more sophisticated medical facilities."

"But, Alex…you can't just leave everything you've accomplished in Boston to move here."

"Of course I can," he answered promptly. Confidently. "During the past weeks, I've slowly come to realize that there are plenty of doctors in the East. More cardiologists than you can shake an EKG at. I'll probably spend some time traveling back there occasionally for consultations and seminars and to visit my friends—but I want to make my home here. With you. If you'll have me."

"You're sure?" She wanted it so badly she could hardly speak. Her words were barely audible, even to her.

"I'm sure. I've been miserable without you, Carly. I love you. I've given everything I had to my practice in Boston, and now I think I deserve a life of my own. A wife. A family. I think between the two of us we can manage to raise a child or two as well as take care of the locals. Don't you think?" he added with an uncharacteristic vulnerability that illustrated just how important her answer was to him.

The tears she'd been holding back for so long spilled unchecked down her face. "I love you, Alex."

"I love you," he answered. "Will you marry me, Carly?"

He knew what he was asking, she realized in wonder. He knew exactly what he was giving up and what he stood to gain in return. What they both stood to gain.

This time she could finally give him the answer she most wanted to give. "Yes."

He broke into a smile that magically mended her broken heart. "You'll never regret this, Carly. And I promise you, I won't, either. This is where I was meant to be."

She brought his mouth to hers again, sealing the deal with a long, healing kiss.

When they finally broke apart, Alex sighed deeply, a sound that was a release of tension as well as an expression of relief. "Let's go inside and tell Betty," he said. "I'm freezing out here."

Laughing softly, Carly took his arm and drew him toward her house.

One very eligible bachelor doctor had just been taken permanently off the market.

* * * * *

Here's a preview of next month's

World's Most

Eligible Bachelors

Theo Petrakis,
the tycoon built like a mythical god from

THE GREEK TYCOON
by
Suzanne Carey

Esme Lord had the beach to herself and, taking off her robe, she decided abruptly to wear nothing at all. Seconds later, her bra and panties lay atop her robe and towel in a little heap and she was slipping naked into the water of the Aegean. Cool but balmier by the moment, it tugged and pulled at her as she waded deeper and then made for an offshore vantage point with smooth, assured strokes. The feeling of swimming that way, in nothing but her satin skin, was matchless, incandescent....

Abruptly, strong, callused hands gripped her ankles, pulling her beneath the water's surface. At least, she prayed they were hands and not the tentacles of an octopus. Struggling to free herself, she found herself dragged against a powerful male body. Shock coursed through her when she realized that her captor, too, was naked—a modern-day Zeus or Apollo stripped for action with an incautious mermaid.

Reason suggested her attacker could be just one person. "Theo Petrakis, please...let go of me!" she gasped, managing to free herself.

It was as if she hadn't spoken a word of protest. His wet hair plastered to his head as he appeared in front of her just long enough to draw breath, he dragged her down, imprisoning her in his powerful arms and pressing his male attributes forthrightly against her. Rough and sweet, his mouth claimed hers as the bubbles of their breath raced buoyantly toward the surface.

Esme found herself gazing into Theo's eyes as they trod water and filled their lungs. His hair loose and dripping about his face, he grinned at her.

Belated indignation rose in a flood. "What in God's name did you think you were doing?" she sputtered. "Let go of me!"

The little grooves that framed his mouth deepened slightly. "Only if you promise not to leave me alone on such a beautiful night."

In truth, the night was exquisite. She didn't *want* to leave. Though Theo Petrakis was a confirmed heartbreaker and *Prominence Magazine*'s latest world's most eligible bachelor, he might be able to teach her something—about men, maybe about herself. The stunned moments of intimacy she'd shared with him had been the most voluptuous she'd ever experienced.

"If you can manage to keep your hands to yourself, I suppose there wouldn't be any harm in us swimming together for a while," she temporized.

To Esme's surprise, it felt safe to be with him in the sea as long as they weren't touching. Thanks to the cloak of night and saltwater, the limits she'd imposed, she found their nakedness tolerable, even comfortable.

As they swam and talked, a distant roll of thunder hinted that a shower—rare in early summer—might be in the offing. Soon there was a more imminent rumble and Theo suggested they head for shore. "The sea can be brilliant when there's a storm approaching,'' he said. ''Though I hate to cut our swim short, I don't want either of us to get hurt by lightning.''

A short time later, they were splashing onto the little beach. ''Don't look,'' Esme pleaded, hastily snatching up her towel.

''And miss Aphrodite rising from the sea?'' He shook his head as if to suggest she was asking the unthinkable. ''What red-blooded man could resist?''

Wrapping her towel around herself as quickly as she could and scooping up her robe and underwear in a kind of bundle, she avoided glancing at him. He didn't make a big deal of his nakedness. Fastening a towel about his hips, he offered her a hand up the steps.

Instead of wishing her a courteous ''good night'' when they reached the terrace and strolling off in the direction of the master suite, Theo put his arms around her as the first fat raindrops of the shower they'd been expecting started to fall. To her dismay, an unsuccessful attempt to free herself caused her towel to slip. She found herself pressed against his muscular body from shoulder to waist.

''I've been longing to kiss you...on dry land... since you arrived in Greece this afternoon looking so disoriented from your journey,'' he confided in a whisper as the downpour accelerated. ''Promise you won't scream and wake everybody up if I indulge myself.''

Apparently the question was a rhetorical one. Before she could answer it, he'd lowered his mouth to hers. Warm and tangy with the sea's taste, his tongue entered her mouth, as if to ravage her innermost sweetness. Rain fell like a curtain. Rivulets ran down her cheeks like tears. Droplets clung to his thick, dark lashes.

If she'd had a few more seconds in which to prepare for his sensual onslaught, she might not have clung to him as she did. Or given in so helplessly. As it was, her knees turned to jelly. Her considerable willpower evaporated. Waves of pleasure broke over her, disarming her usually keen defenses.

Reason warned she had to stop him, before she made a fool of herself. "Please..." she begged, drawing a ragged breath. "You mustn't...."

Echoing a low roll of thunder, his murmur of dissent was sweetly reasonable. "Why not, *krysi mou,* if it's what we both want?"

Somehow she managed to pull up her towel and scrape her wet hair back from her face. "No offense, but I'll be here only briefly. I can't afford to get involved," she protested.

She hadn't counted on his persevering nature. "Who said anything about involvement...yet?" he asked. "If it's meant to be, it will. Meanwhile, the brevity of your visit gives us all the more reason to seize the moment."

He was a confirmed ladies' man, according to *Prominence Magazine*. If she let him, he'd coax her between the sheets, to her shame and his ultimate disappointment.

"Please...don't even *talk* that way," she begged, backing up and putting some distance between them. "I'm not the type of woman to get mixed up in a short-term affair. I've enjoyed swimming with you, and I appreciate your hospitality. But that's going to be the extent of our relationship!"

Not waiting for a reply, she raced up the steps to the second-floor gallery and took refuge in her room.

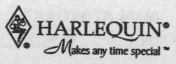